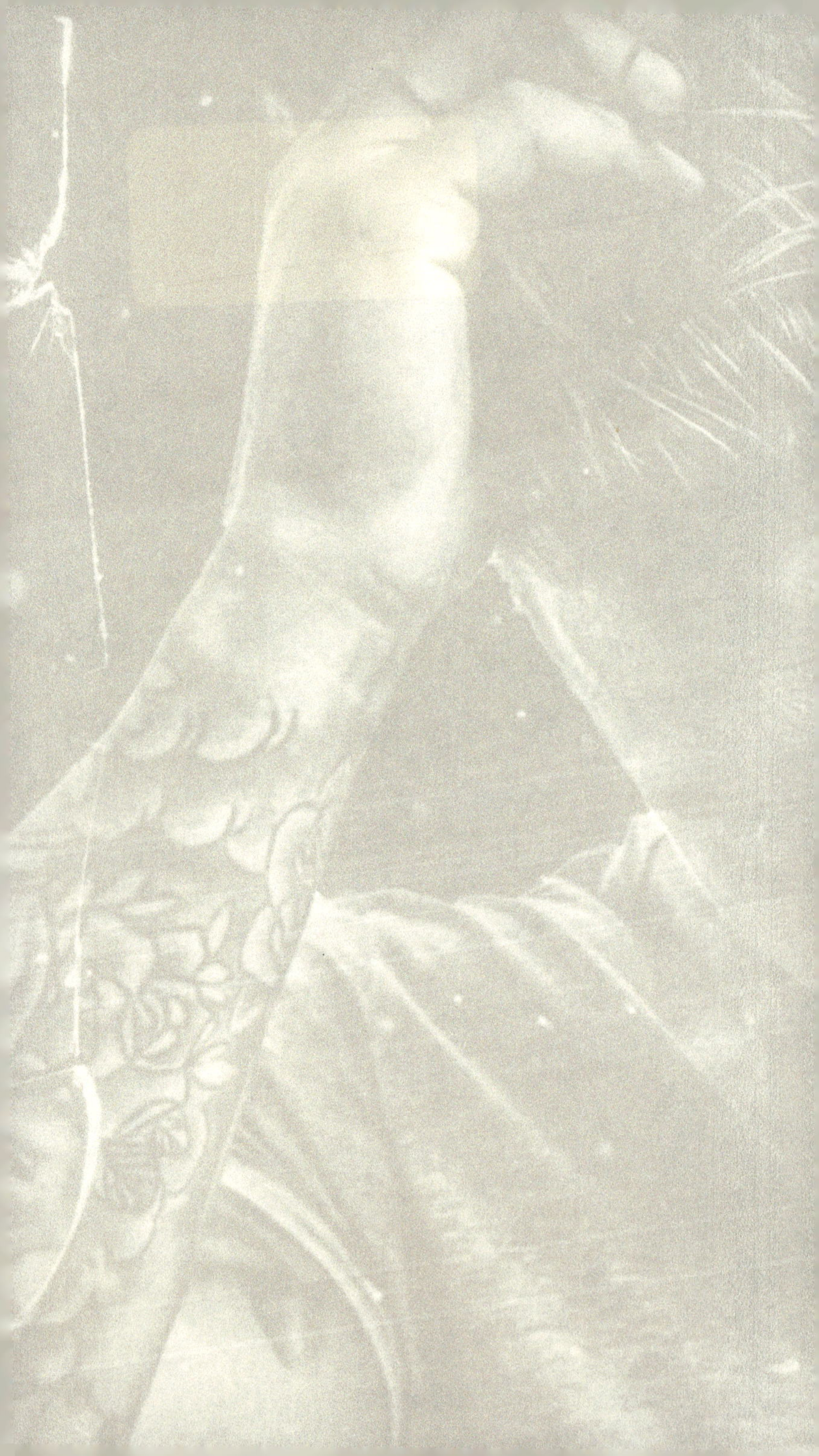

Lennox

RETRIBUTION KINGS BOOK 1

ELLA MILES

Retribution Kings Series

Lennox (Book 1)
Rialta (Book 2)

Hayes (Book 3)
Lilith (Book 4)

Gage (Book 5)
Nova (Book 6)

The Retribution Kings Series is a spinoff of the Retribution Games Series. If you want to read Beckett and River's story, start with Mistaken Hero

CHAPTER 1

Lennox

"WE NEED TO SPEAK—ALONE," I say, staring into the eyes of a monster. By all accounts, this man wants me and my friends dead. I shouldn't be here. I shouldn't be considering what I'm about to do. But even monsters have their weaknesses, and I know exactly how I'm going to exploit his to get what I want.

Unblinking, the monster's dark orbs stare back. The whites of his eyes aren't visible—just dark pupils. He doesn't reveal at all what's going through his head or even if he fully realizes who I am. We've interacted before, but to him I'm just a minion doing Beckett's bidding. I'm not a player in this game, not a leader, so therefore, I'm a nobody to him.

The men around him draw their guns and aim them at me. I shouldn't have been able to get past the other guards and security system, but I did. That makes me dangerous in their eyes.

There is no reason Vincent Corsi should take this meeting; he's a powerful mafia leader. But I'm not going to reveal my hand unless he talks one on one.

I stare Corsi down, silently imploring him to meet with me in private. What I have to discuss is going to be well worth his time and the risk of meeting me without his security.

His eyes skim me up and down like a predator stalking his prey, making it even more obvious that he doesn't actually see me as a threat. Maybe he shouldn't. I have very little power. I have no army of men that will follow me. My combat skills are proficient, but others are better. I don't have a lot of money to pay people to attack him. It's just me.

But something in my gaze makes him decide I'm worth taking a chance on. With the slightest gesture of his hand, the men all lower their guns and file out of the room.

"This better be good," Corsi says, sitting behind his mahogany desk with a glass of whiskey in one hand. He doesn't offer me a drink or even motion for me to take a seat, but then again, I'm not his guest. I'm an intruder who just showed how incompetent his men are.

I take a seat in front of him anyway and grab the bottle of whiskey, helping myself to a glass from the corner of his desk.

His jaw twitches as I pour myself some of his Johnnie Walker Blue, but he doesn't shoot me or tell me to stop. The man has a reputation for being ruthless and killing men for less, but he also respects a man for having some guts around him.

"You have a problem," I say leaning back in my chair.

"I have many problems. Get to the point before I eliminate the one sitting in my office."

I smirk. "I want to marry your daughter."

Corsi freezes. I don't know what he was expecting me to say, but it wasn't that.

It gives me a minute to study the man. Corsi can't be much past fifty, but the years of pain and loss he's suffered have really taken a toll on him. His hair is practically all grey, sunspots cover his skin, and deep wrinkles crinkle his forehead, eyes, and mouth. Those dim eyes are sunken into his head like he hasn't slept for years.

"You want to marry Rialta Corsi?" he asks.

"Yes, I want to marry her."

He narrows his eyes, trying to read my mind and motivation. But I won't let him see past my hard exterior. No one gets to know my real reasoning for this decision. No one gets to know my tragic history. No one but me.

"Why would I ever agree to that?"

"It's the best solution to your problem. The man you chose to do it fell for your adopted daughter instead. And as much as you'd like to force him to marry Rialta, you won't. You love River as much as you love Rialta, and you won't take away her happiness. But you can't wait any longer to get Rialta married."

He frowns. "I can take as much time as I please."

I shake my head. "You can't. You're tired of doing the job. You're ready to pass down the torch to new blood." I pause. "And cancer is coming quickly for you. I've seen your medical records. You need your legacy secured before you go."

His face boils red. "I can do this job as long as I want! I don't need one of Beckett's guard dogs coming in and telling me I need to step down. I may be dying, but I won't go as quickly as you'd like. I have years left."

"I don't have to tell you to step down because you already know it's the truth. It's what you want to do. You need Rialta married. You need Rialta safe. You need your legacy protected. And then you need to retire and live what's left of your life in peace." I take a slow sip of my drink, not letting him see the fear beating through me.

I have no idea if what I'm doing is the smart move, but I

have to try. It's the best way to protect everyone I love—Beckett, River, Hayes, Gage, and even Rialta.

War will continue without Rialta married and the chain of leadership established. The Corsi men need a strong leader, Rialta needs a protector, and I need power I've never had.

"What about the Retribution Kings? You're just going to abandon them? Because you can't do both. You can't lead my men and still be a Retribution King," Corsi says.

"I will gladly relinquish my membership with the Retribution Kings. My loyalty will be to the Corsi men."

"You'll have to change your name to Corsi. None of my men will follow your lead if you aren't willing to take the blood oath. This isn't how it's usually done. For generations, the role passed on through blood from father to son."

He pauses as if the next part hurts him to say. "But my son was killed, along with one of my daughters and my wife —leaving me Rialta. I should marry her to someone within the family, but I won't do that to her. There is no one worthy of her in our family."

I suspect he won't ever think anyone is worthy of Rialta. But it's still shocking that he hasn't found a man within his ranks he trusts. I suspect it's because he thinks one of his own men is a traitor. He thinks one of his men killed his children and wife. He thinks one of his own men has been trying to kill Rialta her entire life.

He doesn't trust them. Beckett gained his trust, but then he fell for the wrong woman. He fell for River instead of Rialta.

Corsi doesn't trust anyone. But he knows what has to be done, so he'll agree to this. He doesn't have much choice.

"My name already is Corsi as far as I'm concerned. I'll take whatever blood oath you want me to take. I want to be a leader of a strong organization like yours. The Retribution Kings have failed me too many times. I want this. I was born to lead. I know I'd make a good mob boss and husband for your daughter."

Corsi doesn't say anything. He's back to just staring at me, trying to read my mind. But he won't be finding the truth. No one knows the darkest secrets of my soul, and he sure as hell won't figure it out in this meeting.

Protecting Beckett, Ri, Hayes, and Gage are only a small part of my reasoning. But even if that was my only motivation for marrying Rialta and becoming a powerful mob boss, it would be more than enough.

Corsi does know what I'm protecting. My true loyalty is to my friends that are more like family.

"What makes you worthy of my daughter?" His stern look tells me this is the question he cares most about. He doesn't care about the Corsi organization. He doesn't care about my leadership skills. He cares about his daughter. I respect him for that.

"I'm not worthy of your daughter. No person alive is, but I hope with time I will prove worthy of her. I will say this, though: I'm a skillful fighter, intelligent, level-headed, calm, disciplined, focused, and honorable. And above all—I'm fiercely protective. I've protected my brothers Hayes and Gage more times than I can count.

"You've seen how I've already protected Beckett, Ri, and Rialta. If you are in my circle, I'll protect you with my life too. I know you want Beckett and Ri to continue protecting Rialta. I've already worked with them, so we'll continue to be a good team to keep her safe. Hayes and Gage are loyal to me and will help protect her as well. I promise you Rialta will be safe with me. I'll never hurt her or let anyone else hurt her. I'll protect her with my life."

It's not a lie, but it's also not the whole truth.

Vincent Corsi knows that. *Is it enough to convince him?*

"I've tried to find a man for Rialta before. I held a contest, a competition where men were willing to risk their lives to have her. Beckett won, but he didn't love her. The only way a man will truly protect her with his life is if he loves her."

My eyes widen in shock, and my mouth falls agape. I wasn't expecting to have to profess my love for Rialta. "I... um...I..." I stutter, unsure of how to convince him that I love Rialta.

"I know you don't love her, but I hope that changes. So my challenge to you is to figure out how to love her. That is the only way I will let you marry her, the only way I'll turn this job over to you someday."

"And if I don't convince you I'm in love with her?" I ask, apprehensive of what he's going to say.

"Then you can try to persuade me in a different way— by finding the man responsible for the deaths of my children and wife. It's the biggest threat to Rialta—find him and bring him to me. Then convince her to marry you and produce an heir together. Only then will I step down and give you my job."

"So my options are: prove that I love her or find the man responsible for your family's destruction? A man that no one has been able to find for twenty years?"

Vincent Corsi nods with a slim smile. "Yes. I don't know why you really want this, but I don't care as long as Rialta is taken care of. She will be protected if you fall in love with her, or she will be taken care of if you eliminate the one man who wants her dead. Either way, she'll be safe."

I swallow the hard lump in my throat.

"Falling in love with Rialta or finding your enemy will

take time. It might be a long time for Rialta to be unmarried and unprotected. The men might grow restless and try to prove themselves worthy of being your heir. A civil war could be started again in the meantime."

I need this settled as soon as possible. I don't have time to deal with his ridiculous stipulations.

Corsi nods. "Which is why you'll be married as soon as it can be arranged."

I sigh, relieved at how easily my plan came together.

"But my conditions remain. If you want to take over my job, then you must fall in love with Rialta and produce an heir or kill the man who wants to end the Corsi line. You have one year. If you fail, I'll kill you. You'll have to take an oath at your wedding in front of my men, vowing as much."

My heart beats erratically. This just became a suicide mission. I can't win. I can't fall in love with Rialta, and finding and killing her mysterious enemy is impossible. Producing an heir with her might just be the only part I can muster.

One year.

Being married to her with access to the Corsi men for a year should be enough; it has to be. But when my time is up, I'll be hunted by some of the most dangerous men in the world.

"Do we have a deal?" Corsi asks me.

I down the rest of the expensive whiskey in one gulp, knowing I have my work cut out for me. There's no way I'll ever fall in love again. It was too painful the first time.

I have no idea how I'm going to be able to find this mystery man, either. One year and then I die if I fail.

I can't fail.

I have to find a way to do the impossible.

I don't have a choice.

I slam my empty glass on the table.

"You have a deal."

"Good, then I'll announce your engagement, and you'll be married within the week. The clock's ticking—one year."

I stand and walk away before I think too hard about the deal I just made and how it will probably be the end of me.

CHAPTER 2

Lennox

I LOOK up at the skyscraper disappearing between the dark clouds hanging low tonight, blocking out all the stars. A flash of lightning lights up the sky before rescinding back into the gloominess.

I hesitate for a second on the sidewalk, dreading going up to Ri and Beckett's apartment to meet Rialta. She needs to hear from me that I'm the man she is to marry. I don't owe her a lot, but I owe her that.

I start walking toward the lobby door when a woman slips out. I don't think anything of her, but then I get a flash of her dark wavy hair and recognize her.

I halt and wait for Ri and Beckett to follow her out, but soon she's halfway down the block and still alone.

Jesus, she's not going to make my life easy. She's not supposed to go anywhere without a security escort. It's only been a few hours since I agreed to marry her, and she's already breaking all the rules. I'll be lucky if I get her down the aisle next week in one piece.

I quickly text Ri and Beckett with an update before setting off after Rialta. I don't know what Corsi has told them yet, but I should talk to Rialta before talking to Ri and Beckett.

Jogging, I could easily catch up to Rialta, but I take my time to see what I can learn about her. I want to know where she's going in the middle of the night. If I'm lucky, it will help me convince Corsi or Rialta of our love. If I'm really lucky, their enemy will reveal himself, and I can be the hero.

I shake my head at the ridiculousness of it all.

Rialta is walking fast in heels and a flowy black dress. Even without a jacket, she doesn't seem bothered by the chill in the air from her speed walk.

I keep my distance in the shadows, even though I want to race to her and lecture her about walking alone at night. Even if she didn't have a killer after her, it wouldn't be wise to walk alone at night on the streets of Chicago as a young woman without any way to protect herself. But I'm too curious to see what she's doing to stop her yet.

A Corvette screeches to a stop next to her.

Shit.

I'm nearby but not close enough to intervene. I take off in a sprint and pull my gun out, but before I can do anything, a man's arm pulls her into the passenger side of the Corvette and speeds off.

I run at full burst, at least hoping to follow them long enough to see where he might be going. I study the car carefully, memorizing every detail to aid in a search later.

I haven't even married her yet, and I've already let her get kidnapped and probably killed. Vincent Corsi will kill me for this. Ri will be devastated at losing the only semblance of a sister she's ever had. And war will start again in this city like never before.

The Corvette turns the corner, and dread fills my heart —I lost them.

If this is the man who has been trying to eliminate her

entire family since before she was born, Rialta will most likely be dead before I can find her.

I pull out my phone and dial Ri's number as I keep running to the block, hoping I can see which way they've turned.

I can't believe my eyes.

The Corvette has stopped a couple of blocks up on the side of the road.

It's not too late.

I hang up before Ri answers. Sticking to the shadows, I move swiftly down the street toward the parked car. They could speed off again at any moment, but I don't want the man driving to spot me either.

Finally, I approach the car, ducking down so the driver can't see me until the last second. Popping up and peering in the driver's side window, I aim my gun at where the driver should be, but the entire front row is empty.

Did they get out of the car?

I glance around, trying to figure out where he might have taken her, when the corner of my eye catches a flash of movement in the backseat.

My heart sinks.

She's alive, but I'm still going to die for failing her. The man is on top of her. She's pinned to the seat beneath him as he thrusts in and out of her—taking what isn't his.

My teeth grind together and my feral growl shoots through the streets as I break the window.

"Get. Off. Her," I yell with my gun pointed at his head.

"Don't hurt her," he says, his voice shaky. "I have money. You can have it all. I'll do whatever you want; just don't hurt her."

My nostrils flare. "Don't hurt her? I'm not the one hurting her."

"I'm—I'm not hurting her," his squeaky voice revealing

his inexperience. He's probably the same age as me, but our lives have led us to very different places. I haven't been a boy since I was ten, and he's a full-grown man-child.

He's not the secret threat to the Corsis, but he could be working for him or some other rival gang. If it wouldn't traumatize Rialta, I would have already blown his brains out. But it's also the responsible thing to torture him for information before I kill him.

"Get out of the car. Now."

"Oh-okay." He's trembling—the coward. He can rape a woman—hurt her, but he'll be pissing his pants soon and begging for his life. He can dole out pain but can't take any. He's the worst kind of man, and I'll enjoy making him scream.

I give him room to get out of the car, and it gives me the opportunity to really look at Rialta.

Her dress is hiked up to her waist, and her legs are spread open. I look at her face, trying to comfort her with my eyes, although I don't do emotion. I'm terrible at consoling anyone.

Her eyes flash wild, and her nostrils flare in a fury I've never seen before from her.

Good, she's going to need that rage to recover from this.

I failed at preventing her pain, but I'm not going to let her suffer a second longer than she needs to. I yank her out of the car, pulling down her dress to cover her as best as I can.

She starts flailing—trying to strike me with her fists and bite me with her teeth.

Fuck, she doesn't see who I am in the darkness. She doesn't realize I'm here to save her. That or she's already so traumatized that she's still living in the nightmare.

I focus solely on her, not worrying about the boy, who I can easily track and kill after I get her to safety. I ignore the sound of him running down the sidewalk as I wrap my arms around her.

"Get off of me!" she screams, trying to strike me again but failing.

I make a mental note to teach her better self-defense soon. What she's doing now wouldn't fight off weak old man, let alone most of the men in our world.

"You're safe; I've got you. It's Lennox. You're safe, Rialta."

"I'm not fucking safe!" She tries to kick me but ends up kicking the car door instead.

I hold her tighter, worried she's going to hurt herself.

"Rialta, I need you to take a deep breath and calm down. Then I'll let you go."

She kicks one more time and then does as I say. I take a deep breath with her. When she's taken two more breaths and seems to have calmed down, I gently loosen my grip on her.

It's enough for her to finally break free of my hold. "You're an asshole."

I frown. "I just saved your life. I'm sorry I didn't get here sooner. I promise I'll never let that happen again, but you should be thanking me, not calling me an asshole."

"I should be thanking you?" Her eyebrows shoot up.

"Yes, I just pulled a rapist off of you. He probably would have killed you."

She shakes her head incredulously. "You guys and your constant need to save the damsel in distress. I'm not a damsel, and I wasn't in distress."

"Oh, so you had it completely under control as that bastard was thrusting inside you?"

She's in denial. It will hit her soon, and she'll collapse into darkness. I've seen it happen before; it's happened to *me* before.

"He's not a bastard."

My eyes narrow. I replay the situation again in my mind, realizing too late what she's going to say.

"That man wasn't raping me. He's my *boyfriend*." She crosses her arms and swings her hip as she waits for my apology.

Well, she's not going to get one from me. I did nothing wrong. She snuck out without telling anyone, and she sure as hell shouldn't be having a boyfriend. She almost married one of my best friends.

"Well, I hope you enjoyed your last fuck with him."

She glares at me. "That wasn't my last fuck with him."

"It was, actually."

Her eyes flick across mine, trying to understand the meaning behind my words and what I'm even doing here. Her eyes widen slowly as the realization hits her too.

"I'll propose under more romantic circumstances soon, but you and I are arranged to be married in a week."

CHAPTER 3

Rialta

FIVE DAYS until I marry Lennox. That is how my life is going to be divided now—days I have left of my own life and days I'm a prisoner. As much as I hope this wedding will be called off, I know deep in my heart that it won't be.

I could run away.

I could refuse.

My father, Vincent Corsi, loves me and has done everything he can to protect me, but when it comes to this, he won't give me a choice. He won't let me refuse. He'll force me down the aisle if it comes to it.

He'll force me because it's what's expected of him: find a successor to run the family business and marry me off to him. Then have me bred like a fucking farm animal, ideally impregnated with a boy, who would then carry on the business after Lennox dies.

But Vincent will also force me because he loves me. There is nowhere I could run, nowhere I could hide that I would ever be safe. He hid me away for a while, but it could have never lasted. Vincent has decided that Lennox is the best protection he can find me, so Vincent will force me to marry Lennox even if it means I hate my father for the rest of my life.

I'm tired of hating so many people in my life, though. So if this is what my father wants, if this is what my sister River thinks is best, then so be it. I'll do it. I'll marry Lennox Crane, but I won't be happy about it. And until the day of the wedding, I'm still going to hold out hope and do everything I can in my power to convince everyone that this marriage is going to end in shambles.

Beckett walks up to the hostess stand, while River and I wait back. They're both tense as she and I stand in the foyer of one of the top steakhouses in the city. I don't care about the steak, but the view from the top floor of this high-rise is to die for.

When I glance from Beckett to River, I'm afraid that's exactly what they think is going to happen. *We'll all be dead in a matter of minutes.*

"No one is going to attack us here. And if they do, you and Beckett will kick their asses. Stop worrying," I say.

River nods, her jaw tight as Beckett turns back to her and grimaces. They hold each other's gaze a second too long. There's obviously something going on with them, but I don't know what. And it's clear neither of them feels like sharing.

Shivers creep up my spine. They've always been cautious, especially when it comes to my safety, but they've taken things to a whole new level recently. They don't trust anyone—definitely not any of Vincent's men, not even their friends.

Good, welcome to my world. I don't trust anyone but them, either.

While we wait for the hostess, Beckett steps to River's side and pulls her into his chest with his arm and residual limb, comforting her. It's an unusual display of affection when they are working. Usually, they're all business working as my only trusted security guards.

For a second, I look at them with envy even though their life has been anything but easy. Beckett lost an arm, and River lost her life. They both almost lost each other numerous times. But it must be nice to be able to love the person they care most about so openly.

The hostess gestures to us and leads us through the restaurant to where a long rectangular table has been set up in place of the usual intimate tables for two or four. Normally the restaurant would be packed with people, but my father rented out the entire place for the night. The only guests here are sitting at a single long table.

We are the last to arrive by design. It gives Beckett and River time to observe everyone and look for any threats. But it also means there are only three seats left at the table. The one I'm expected to sit in is clear—the one next to *him*.

I refuse to take that seat, though. I'd rather sit anywhere else. It's petty, but I don't care—if it's a decision I can make, I'm going to make it.

I'm about to sit in the seat furthest away from Lennox, when Beckett suddenly slides into the seat, limiting my choices.

I practically shriek at him, but he ignores me and immediately starts talking to Hayes next to him. I'm glad I didn't end up married to Beckett like my father originally wanted. He's quickly become like an annoying older protective brother. He's fucking drool-worthy, sure, but I could see from the second I came back that he was in love with River. And no matter how attracted I was to him, I would never hurt my sister. Even if she isn't a sister by blood, she means everything to me and more.

I shake my head and am about to sit in the middle seat

when River beats me to it. She at least has an apologetic look on her face and mouths 'sorry.'

I sigh. I should relinquish control and accept my fate. My life would be much more enjoyable if I did. I'd be a powerful wife of a mafia boss. I'd be pampered and live in a big mansion. I'd have people protecting me. I wouldn't have to work. I could draw and paint every day and not worry about a thing.

I sit down in the seat, feeling everyone's eyes on me as I hold my head high, not daring to look at the man to my left.

That would be the easy choice—surrendering. My chest tightens at the thought of giving up freedom for protection. Freedom for safety. I'd rather risk my life for a chance at love than ever surrender.

I'm not the same girl I was when my father sent me away for my safety.

One day I was a normal girl, living with adopted parents, having nightmares every night about a past I barely remembered. I was dating boys, learning to drive, and figuring out which colleges I wanted to attend. I was learning to draw, spending afternoons chilling with friends, and evenings working at a bar. And then the next thing I knew, I was thrown back into a life of menacing men who treat me like my only worth is in marrying and breeding to give them heirs who will eventually become dangerous men too.

That little girl before I left was scared, meek, and timid. I was indecisive and loyal. But I've changed, and soon, everyone is going to know just how much.

Vincent is sitting at the head of the table, and his are the only eyes I haven't felt on me. Lennox is to his right— already seated at the right hand of the devil.

I wish my father would look at me—show disappointment in me. But he loves me too much to ever be disappointed in me. He wasn't even upset when River fell in love with the man he picked out for me. For once, I wish he would be pissed at me. It might make me feel worthy, like I'm not his little princess he expects perfection from. I'm a flawed human who wants to follow her own heart like every other man here gets to.

Vincent opens his mouth, and the room falls silent. He didn't ask for attention, he demanded it, and he got it. It's one of the things I respect most about my father. He's ruthless and powerful, and he's earned every bit of his position.

A dozen eyes look at him and listen eagerly for him to speak. Most are the highest-ranking men my father trusts, here with their wives. The rest are Lennox's men.

I don't look at my father as he speaks; I look at the men. Any one of them could be the reason I spent over a decade living with strangers. As much as I know River and Beckett will protect me—I want revenge. I want to hurt whoever took my youth from me. If it wasn't for them, I would have had years to convince my father to let me choose my own husband. He wouldn't feel the rush to have me married and produce an heir.

"Thank you all for coming. As you know, we have much to celebrate tonight. The announcement will be public soon enough, but I wanted my close circle, the people I consider my family, to be the first to know and congratulate the couple. My daughter, Rialta, is engaged to be married to Lennox Crane."

Vincent turns to Lennox. "Lennox has agreed to take the blood oath at the wedding, which will ensure that he is ready to be one of us. But in the meantime, welcome Lennox into our family and join me in congratulating the soon-to-be newlyweds."

Blood oath?

I'm not sure I want to know what that is. Some stupid ritual that will supposedly ensure his loyalty, not that it's stopped someone among us from continually trying to kill me.

Vincent lifts his drink, as does everyone else at the table, and they drink to us. Lennox doesn't look at me, and I don't look at him. We haven't talked since two nights ago when Lennox tried to save me from what he thought was a kidnapping and rape, when really it was just me trying to meet up with my boyfriend.

I don't know why Lennox agreed to this, except to gain power. He doesn't like me. In fact, I don't think Lennox likes anyone. He's the grumpy one, the responsible one, and evidently, the power-hungry one.

Cheers ring out across the room, mostly from Lennox's friends. Vincent's men are skeptical. Most of them are Vincent's age and married, but any one of them would jump at the chance to take Vincent's position. They're unlikely to trust a newcomer, even though Vincent thinks this is for the best. This dinner is as much about seeing if anyone leaks my fiancé's identity to the outside world. If someone does, it brings us a little closer to finding the possible mole in our ranks.

I look at Lennox out of the corner of my eye. He doesn't take a sip of his drink, and he still won't look at me. He stoically sits there in his blue suit, which clashes with my emerald dress. It figures we can't even dress complimentary—this marriage is doomed before it's started.

But he does look good in that suit. His reddish brown hair is textured in a long French crop, swooping just over his suit-matching blue eyes. Tattoos sneak out along his collar and down his hands. He looks young but intimidating at the same time.

His eyes finally glance at me, realizing he should look at the woman he's supposed to marry. To him, I'm just a small part of what he has to put up with to get what he really wants—my father's power.

I narrow my gaze at him, his eyes turning darker, more cynical. He's agitated just looking at me with his twitching jaw and tense fist.

"You could at least pretend to like me when everyone's watching," I whisper through a fake smile.

"Why? Everyone knows I'm not in love with you. And they'll respect me more for not pretending, you spoiled brat."

I roll my eyes and vow to make him pay for seeing me as a posh princess. I may have all the money I could ever desire, but most of my life I grew up with nothing. I'd gladly trade in my princess title for a little bit of liberation. My mind whirls with torturous ideas. One in particular solidifies in my head, but I'm not sure I'm brave enough to do it. We'll see how dinner goes.

I gulp down the glass of my favorite wine in front of me, but it won't be nearly enough to get me through this dinner. Nor will wine help me teach Lennox the lesson he desperately needs. So instead, I snatch his whiskey and down it before he can protest.

I expect another brat comment or to be scolded in some way for stealing his drink—a reaction, any reaction at all. But Lennox doesn't even bat an eye. He was expecting me to behave like a child, which somehow annoys me even more.

River looks at me with raised eyebrows but doesn't admonish me either. She may be like a big sister to me, but thankfully she's not the type to tell me what to do unless it involves my safety. Drinking excessively may be stupid, but it most likely won't cause me any harm other than a horrible hangover in the morning.

Lennox flags down one of the waiters. "Two whiskeys and another glass of wine."

The waiter nods and then leaves.

I squint at him in confusion.

When the waiter returns, he places one whiskey in front of Lennox and the other in front of me, along with a refill of my wine. I just stare at my two drinks. I don't know if I'm happy with my soon-to-be husband or furious.

"Why did you do that?" I ask.

He sighs. "You getting wasted helps us both. I don't have to talk to you, and you won't even have to remember tonight."

"You're a fucking prick."

He shrugs. "Doesn't change the fact that we're getting married."

"It does if I have anything to say about it."

I pull out my phone and send a quick message, deciding to put my plan in motion after all. Then I turn my attention to River.

"Do you want my advice?" River asks me, looking from me to Lennox.

"Nope, not even a little."

"Okay, then." She smiles at me, trying to hide her own concern. There was a time we were inseparable and bluntly honest with each other. We often didn't even have to speak because we already knew the other's thoughts. That bond was broken when we were forced to spend much of our childhood and teenage years apart.

"Are you going to talk to me about whatever is going on between you and Beckett?" I spit back.

River frowns. "There is nothing going on between Beckett and me. We are happier than ever."

"Bullshit. You two are more paranoid than ever."

River's mouth opens to speak for a split second—ready to spill whatever secret she's hiding, but it snaps shut quickly, and she shakes her head.

I nod, understanding. It's going to take time for us to get that trust back, if we ever do. Even so, she's still the person I trust most in the world. Still, neither of us is ready to spill our secrets.

River and I make idle chit-chat through dinner. I ignore Lennox, and he seems happy to be doing the same. *Well, that's not true—Lennox is never really happy.*

He always has a scowl of gloom on his face. He thinks he's above everyone else around him, and it's hurting him to have to talk to anyone. He's a moody, surly grump. I don't understand why anyone would want to be his friend. While River, Beckett, Hayes, Gage, and I make jokes and laugh, Lennox sulks.

If I do end up having to marry him, the only positive will be that he probably won't speak to me. We'd live on opposite sides of a grand mansion. The only problem is the whole having to create heirs part.

I shiver at the thought of him touching me, let alone fucking me. At least, that's what I tell myself when my core warms and tingles slightly at the thought. Fucking him wouldn't be the worst travesty, but I'll never admit that out loud.

Vincent pulls out his phone and takes a call. Thankfully, that usually means dinner is about to end. He says something to Lennox and walks into a different room.

As soon as Vincent leaves the room, the table gets rowdier.

Lennox finally turns to me. "Are you ready to leave?"

"I am, but not with you."

"We should be seen leaving together. Of course, we aren't going to the same place."

Thank heavens.

I glance at my phone and see a message—perfect timing.

I nod and let Lennox pull my chair back as I stand, giving the impression of leaving together.

The table looks up at us with amused looks, expecting to see some display of affection between us. If that's what they want, they'll be waiting a long time.

River, Beckett, Hayes, and Gage all stand too and follow us out of the restaurant. Lennox walks by my side but doesn't touch me. For a moment, it does feel like we are equals, but that's not how this works. If I marry him, I will be below him. I will be expected to follow his orders without defiance or opinions at all. I'll be expected to be his obedient wife—a woman at his side with no real power or responsibilities at all except to look pretty and bear his children.

I sigh as we wait in the lobby for the valets to bring our cars around. My stomach is rattling with anxiety as I wait for my moment to act.

Tonight is one step closer to my ill-fated destiny, one step closer to having to marry a man I didn't choose. I don't care how kind, smart, or good-looking Lennox Crane is. I don't care that he saved my life and helped ensure Beckett and River got their happily ever after.

I look over at Lennox, who is looking bored as we wait for our cars. I don't care about any of that. I don't love the man, and I didn't pick him.

I look over at Beckett's hand wrapped around River's stomach, holding her protectively. They look so at peace with each other no matter how the rest of the world is spinning into chaos around them. That's all I want. I want to choose the person I love. I want to choose my own fate.

Our cars appear quickly, and I realize my plan isn't going to happen after all. One of my last chances to have a say in my future is vanishing.

As we all step outside to get into the cars, a Corvette pulls into the drive next to us.

I grin and quickly come to ease. I need to take control of my life back. I need to show Lennox just how bad of an adversary I can be. I need there to be no way he wants to marry me. I need to put a stop to all of this.

I start walking toward the Corvette.

"Rialta, what are you doing?" River asks.

"Taking my future into my own hands." I strut toward the car, surprised no one has stopped me. Especially Lennox —I know he recognizes the car as soon as he sees it. As I approach, the man in the driver's seat gets out with a swagger to his step. He's wearing dark jeans, a black t-shirt, a leather jacket, and shades even though it's dark outside.

He grins at me—clearly as thrilled as I am about my decision. His smirk is infectious, so I smile back and practically sprint toward him. I throw my body around him—arms around his neck, legs around his waist—and I kiss him.

CHAPTER 4

Lennox

I WATCH HER KISS HIM.

I watch how she throws herself at him, wrapping her body around him like she owns him. He grins into the kiss, loving the attention, and that she finally decided to make their relationship public. He doesn't realize her rash decision tonight was probably a death sentence for him, especially with how reckless the other night had been. I was so close to killing him without question.

If Vincent Corsi or any of his top men find out, they *will* kill him. Luckily for him, I don't see any of Corsi's men anywhere in sight. And I doubt killing Rialta's boyfriend would make her like me more. He's safe—for now. Although I'm sure Ri and Gage are already doing a background check, so he may not stay safe from them, depending on what they find.

Rialta runs her hand down his muscular arm. They're muscles you get in the gym, not muscles from learning to survive a fight. Unlike everyone else here, he doesn't have a scar on his body. This man has probably never even punched someone before.

She continues running her hand down his body until she's encouraging him to grab her ass—a public display of affection meant to rile me up.

It's not going to work. I couldn't care less who she's kissing or fucking as long as the guy doesn't hurt her. If he did, I would be the one blamed. I'm supposed to protect her. It's my main mission if I want to become a Corsi man.

My only real problem with this guy is that he's an opponent to winning Rialta's affection. And if I fail to make her love me, I'm a dead man.

I sigh as he eagerly grabs her ass and shoves his wet tongue down her throat. The giggle that leaves her throat is so loud the entire street can hear how fake it is.

"Want me to kill him?" Hayes asks deadpan.

I give him a pinched expression.

"At least let me rough him up a bit, so he'll know who he's dealing with. Look at him; he's just a baby looking for attention and her daddy's money. We can squash this tonight, and he'll never want to come near her again," Hayes continues.

Beckett looks like he wants to murder this guy. He knows he's going to have to babysit this asshole instead of getting his wife home. Ri yawns, and I suspect I know why they're both eager to go home and not deal with this drama.

I don't respond. Everyone seems to agree it's my decision on how to handle the situation. As much as I want to personally pummel the guy until he decides never to touch Rialta again, I'm not going to.

They aren't in love. It's clear she's just using him to get under my skin to try and convince me not to marry her. She doesn't realize this isn't about her, and I could care less. I don't care what she does or who she fucks. I don't care if she's a virgin or not. I don't care about her beyond the deal I made with her father.

The sooner she learns that, the sooner she'll stop acting out and start negotiating what she wants in this marriage. Getting out of it isn't an option for either of us.

But dealing with this asshole is a delicate balance of finding a way to get rid of him, while not making her hate me even more than she already does.

Casually, I walk over to the tangled couple. They don't notice me, too entranced with each other like teenagers making out before one of them sneaks in after curfew.

Without a word, I scoop Rialta up in my arms.

"Hey, put me down!" she yells as I lift her up. Her boyfriend smartly doesn't fight. He doesn't even attempt to hold onto her as I take her away. *Maybe he won't die after all.*

I walk her to my Audi and set her down in the passenger seat. I slam the door without a word to her and then start walking to the driver's side.

"Rialta is staying with me tonight. Beckett and Ri, you can have the night off."

Ri is about to protest, but Beckett whispers something in her ear, and she nods her agreement. She's too tired to quarrel.

"Hayes and Gage, follow behind us. I need to speak to Rialta alone, but keep watch for us."

I don't wait for them to agree; I know they will.

I get into my seat, buckle my seatbelt, and then I start driving. I'm genuinely surprised to find that Rialta already has her seatbelt on and hasn't tried to make a run for it. That little public display of affection was just a show, and she's not really going to fight this. She knows we have no choice but to get married at this point now that her father has announced it. It was just one final act of rebellion.

I don't speak as I drive carefully through the streets of

Chicago. She doesn't ask where we are going or what changed my mind.

I spot Hayes and Gage in the car behind me as I drive, which puts me at ease.

"Can you be driving any slower, grandpa?"

"Giving you time to cool off and lower your libido before we get to my apartment. I wouldn't want you all hot and bothered and accidentally cheat on your boyfriend."

She glares at me. "Don't act like you're not upset that I have a boyfriend I'm regularly seeing while you have no one."

"Okay, I won't act. I don't have to. I'm not upset. I could care less who you fuck."

"Sure, you don't." She studies me closely, looking for any sign of anger, stress, or annoyance. She'll find none. I'm more determined than ever to do what I have to do to protect those I love. And in order to do that, I have to keep her alive—no matter how annoying she is.

She sighs when she doesn't find what she's looking for and instead puts her feet up on my dashboard.

My lips curl as I glare at her.

"Really? My feet on your dash—that's what's annoying to you?"

"This is a very safe car. You putting your feet up where the airbags are isn't safe. You could break your legs if the airbags go off."

She doesn't lower her legs. "You don't care if I break my legs. You just care that I'm getting your precious car dirty."

I slow down even further, ensuring if we got into an accident, the airbags wouldn't go off.

She rolls her eyes but still doesn't remove her legs from the dash.

I lower my speed to under twenty-five miles an hour. I'm

sure Gage and Hayes are confused but will easily guess my actions have something to do with her shenanigans.

She groans at how slow I'm going, but we are both too stubborn to yield. What should have been a half-hour drive takes well over an hour, but we finally arrive at my apartment.

When I park the car in the garage under my apartment building next to Hayes and Gage, they look at me suspiciously.

"Is there a reason you were going so slow?" Hayes asks.

"Yes."

Hayes chuckles, looking from me to Rialta. "I knew it! She's a spitfire. You're going to have your hands full."

I ignore him and head to the elevator. I know I'm going to have my hands full keeping Rialta safe when she's so intent on making that job damn near impossible. Thankfully, Rialta follows without me having to pressure her. Hayes and Gage right behind her, already skilled at boxing her in and making her as hard a target as possible.

Gage has the security system cameras pulled up on his phone, and Hayes has his hand resting on his gun, as do I.

My apartment is safe. We have all the best technology keeping us safe, but you can never be too careful. All it takes is one mistake, and everything would be ruined.

I scan my card and hit the button for the top floor. The elevator starts going up, and Rialta stands in the corner, picking red paint flakes off her nails.

We get to my floor, and Hayes and Gage hurry off first. Rialta goes to step off the elevator when I put my arm in front of her.

"What are you doing?"

"We need to wait until Gage and Hayes give the all-clear before we enter my apartment."

"No one is going to hurt me here."

"You don't know that."

"Can we at least wait in the hallway?"

"No."

"I would think the elevator is far less safe than the hallway. Someone could snap the cord, and we could die."

"The elevator is safe. And if someone is in the apartment, this is the fastest way to escape."

"All clear," Gage yells from down the hallway.

I remove my hand from in front of her chest, and she struts out of the elevator and down the hallway. Gage is holding the door open, and Hayes is waiting in the hallway for us.

I tread behind her.

"We'll be monitoring from my apartment," Gage says.

I nod and then follow Rialta inside as the door falls shut behind me.

Alone at last.

I feel my throat close up at that thought and immediately start to feel claustrophobic with her in my space. I've never shared my apartment with anyone, not even the guys. Suddenly my 900 square foot loft feels like a ten-foot by ten-foot closet with her inside. This is my sanctuary, but with her here, it feels like my own personal hell.

I watch her examine every inch of my space. It's not huge, but it's plenty of space for just me. A brick wall lines one side of the apartment, and slanted windows line the other side. A plushy dark grey couch overlooks the lake outside. Stainless steel kitchen appliances mix in with a handful of dark grey cabinets in the kitchen. Dark metal stairs line the back wall against the brick, leading up to the open loft bedroom lined with shades of grey and attached to a simple en-suite bathroom.

I put my hands in my pockets, waiting for her to say something cruel like how my apartment isn't big enough.

Why isn't there a TV? Why is everything a shade of grey or black? Why don't I have color?

I expect her to tell me we aren't living here after we get married. She wants a penthouse condo that covers an entire floor or a mansion in the suburbs.

Instead, she plops down on the comfy couch and stares out the window at the moon and stars over the lake, not saying anything. Apparently, not hearing her opinion drives me crazier than hearing her whining.

"No snide remarks?" I ask, walking to the kitchen.

"I always knew you were a vampire, so this suits you."

My lips lift in a small smile hidden by the fridge door as I open it. I grab a tray of meats and cheeses from the fridge, a couple of wine glasses from a cabinet, and a bottle of red from the bar cart before walking back to the couch.

"If I was a vampire, I wouldn't have the big windows. Vampires can't walk in the sun."

"Depends what kind of vampire we're talking about—sparkly Twilight vampires, sexy Vampire Diaries vampires, or Dracula vampires." She looks at me for a second. "You're right. You're more of a Dracula—we just need to get you a coffin, and you'd be all set."

I roll my eyes as I set the tray of food down on the ottoman and hand her a glass.

She raises an eyebrow. "You're serving me more alcohol? I thought you'd lecture me about not getting drunk."

I remove the cork and pour us both a glass. "You're already drunk. It doesn't matter if you have another glass. I need one to get through this conversation. And I don't want to listen to you complain about how unfair it is that you don't get to drink if I'm having one. Maybe the cheese and meat tray will offset the alcohol enough for you to listen to me."

"God, you're pleasant. I can't believe no one has wanted

to marry you before now." She grabs a piece of cheese and pops it into her mouth.

I want to respond to her comment, but I'm just happy she's eating something. I can't have her pass out before we talk.

I sit down on the couch next to her, trying to keep my blood from boiling. In a normal world, I would have nothing to do with a woman like Rialta. She's annoying, spoiled, and pretentious. She thinks she's better than everyone else and doesn't mind others risking their lives while she lives carelessly.

I don't know how Corsi expects me to fall in love with her. It's impossible to love someone who gets under my skin so easily. But I don't have an option. Finding the man who wants her dead would be just as impossible. I have to at least try to do both. It's my only chance of surviving.

I should be afraid of Corsi's threat, but if I fail in my mission, I'd rather die anyway. I need this to work. I can't fail.

"The recklessness has to stop," I say in a voice much more serious than I intended, but it grabs her attention in the way I need. This is a serious conversation, and I need her to take it seriously.

"You're not my father, and I'm not a kid. You can't just tell me what to do."

"I'm not telling you what to do. I'm discussing the terms of our arranged marriage with you. And one of my terms is that you can't be reckless anymore."

She crosses her arms and tucks her legs under her on the couch, trying to get as far away from me as possible. "So you're mad about me kissing my boyfriend in front of you and sneaking off with him the other night. I knew you were jealous."

"I'm not jealous. I just don't like you risking the lives of people I care about all so you can parade around like the princess you think you are," I snap.

"I didn't put anyone else's life in jeopardy! It was just a kiss!"

My nostrils flare. "It was more than a kiss, and you know that. You hoped that someone would see and they would change Corsi's mind about our marriage."

"There is nothing dangerous about that."

"No, but there are still plenty of people who want you dead. Plenty of men who would force you into a marriage in order to get power. If anyone thinks our marriage isn't inevitable and completely solid, then you're at risk. And if you're at risk, then people I love, people I thought you loved —Ri, Beckett, Hayes, Gage—they are all at risk of having to put their lives on the line to protect you. They are willing to do that. But don't ask them to when they don't have to."

She frowns, tapping her finger nervously against her forearm. I wait for her smart comeback, but it never comes.

"What else?" she finally asks.

"What else what?"

"What else do you want from me in this arrangement? You don't want me to be reckless. I can't promise that I won't be—it's in my nature. But I do promise I'll think about how my actions put others in danger."

I want to argue for more, but this is a concession for her, so for now, it's enough.

"We get married in a week. No more stunts trying to prevent it from happening. It's going to happen. Neither of us has a choice, not after your father made the announcement tonight. It will make your father look weak if we back out now, and Corsi can't afford to look vulnerable."

She narrows her gaze at me—her dark brown eyes turning vicious. If looks could kill, she'd be tearing out my throat so I could no longer speak of such things like us getting married being inevitable. She still has hope that something will change.

It won't. It *can't*.

But she still has hope, so I need to squash it.

"Five days, actually," she mutters under her breath, correcting me.

"What?" I ask, not sure I heard her.

"We get married in five days, not a week. And what am I getting out of this? So far, I have to be a perfectly behaved Stepford wife. I have to accept my fate as your bride without argument. I have to shut my mouth and pretend I don't have my own thoughts and dreams. What do I get, huh?"

She stands up now, knocking her glass of wine onto my cream rug. She doesn't move to pick it up. She doesn't care.

I get up slowly, setting my glass down carefully, unsure of how to handle her. I walk toward where she's standing at the window, but she whips around to face me before I have a chance to say anything.

"You get power. You get money. You get to control me. You get everything you could ever fucking want! What do I get?" She pushes a finger into my chest, like this arrangement is completely my fault.

Okay, so it mostly is, but only because I didn't have another choice. And if she doesn't marry me, she'll have to marry someone else she hates. She would never get to choose. It makes no difference in her life.

I laugh—I shouldn't. It's not going to help things, but I can't help it.

She goes rigid at my laugh—her eyes bulging and cheeks reddening with rage. "You think this is funny?"

"No, I think you're crazy if you think I'm getting more out of this relationship than you are. I'm marrying you to protect my friends. Beckett would have had to marry you or be killed if I didn't come up with a solution to appease your father. I never wanted to be a leader. I'm a terrible leader. I'm already tired of the responsibility, and I don't even have it yet. Money? I already have enough. And controlling you?" I laugh. "There is no controlling you, sweetheart."

She frowns. "Then why marry me? Why go through with it? Beckett is safe. He already married Ri. Why?"

It comes out as a plea—a plea to save her from having to marry me. But I can't save her. *No one can.*

I shake my head with vacant eyes, not answering her.

"I don't want to control you, Rialta. I want you to be as happy in this marriage as you can be."

"I just want my freedom. That's all I want."

I nod, understanding. "You can have as much freedom as you do now."

She turns and looks out the window pensively, clasping her hands in front of her body. "Except, I don't have any freedom now. I can't marry you, Lennox. There is nothing you can say that will make me go through with it."

I hesitate for just a second, trying to come up with a different way, but it's the only way to disarm her. The only way to ease her hate of me and pry the slightest opening of her heart to me.

"Even if I tell you that you can keep him?"

Her eyes widen with a hint of hope, and I know I have her. I can practically see her heart beating through her chest. *It's too easy.*

"Keep him?" she says so softy.

"Marry me, and I'll let you keep your boyfriend," I say, knowing the gamble I'm playing and hoping it's not going to blow up in my face later. With any luck, he'll fuck up, and she'll realize he's no good for her. I just have to bide my time, and she'll fall into my arms, begging me to erase him from her memory.

CHAPTER 5

Rialta

MY MOUTH FALLS OPEN, and my body sways as I stare at Lennox. I can't believe he just said that.

Lennox nonchalantly stands with his hands in the pockets of his suit, as if he asked me if I wanted another glass of wine or something. But he just dropped a bomb on me.

I don't believe him. All the mob men I've ever seen control their wives with an iron fist. Surely, Lennox will be no different.

"What do you want in this arrangement?" I ask.

"I want you to stop putting yourself and those trying to protect you in danger."

I watch him carefully, waiting for him to say something to which I can't agree.

"I want you to stop fighting this and marry me willingly this Saturday," he goes on.

Metal cages go up around my heart at the thought of being married in five days. I hold my stomach that's churning. Marriage is not something I want—ever. I can't be controlled; I need my freedom.

"I want us to agree on where we'll live. If it's a mansion or—"

"Here," I say.

He pauses, cocking his head to the side.

"I don't want a big mansion. Plus, Hayes and Gage have their own apartments here. It's far enough away from Vincent, but also close enough that we can easily meet up with people when we need to."

"There's only one bedroom here," he says, stone-faced.

I meet his gaze, staring him down, trying to figure out what his endgame is. He's hiding something. But if we do share such a small place together, I'll find out his secrets eventually.

"I have no problem with us staying here. But if it becomes too much for you, then I'm fine moving too," he continues.

I nod, feeling oddly calm here, unlike how I feel about marrying him. It's simple and cozy. It is small, so we'll probably end up killing each other. At least if I can't prevent the marriage from happening, I can hope for a quick divorce.

"Of course, when we have a baby, we'll want to move."

"Baby?" I squeak.

"Yes, *baby*," Lennox rubs his forehead as if I give him a headache at how slow he has to explain things to me. As if I'd never considered the word. *It's not the word I have a problem with.*

"I'm in love with Kit. How can I have a baby with you when I love him? How could I live with myself if I have a relationship with him but fuck you? I can't do that to someone I love."

"You're in love with him?" he says with a look that radiates his arrogance. He thinks I don't know my own heart—that I'm too young and naive to know what love is.

"Yes, I am," I say forcefully, irritated again.

"Hmmm," he says, turning with a wide stance to look out the window as rain gently taps on the glass and a streak of light flashes across the sky.

"Don't 'hmmm' me, talk to me."

"I don't think you want to hear what I have to say."

"I don't, but you're going to tell me anyway."

Lennox turns and faces me with a smug amusement in his eyes. He likes getting under my skin; it fascinates him.

"This is all just a game to you," I say.

With a harsh squint and puffed-out chest, he says, "You have no idea how serious I take this arrangement. You have no idea what the stakes are."

"So enlighten me!"

He turns his head, staring back out the window with an unnatural stillness. Whatever or whoever he's thinking about isn't going to be revealed tonight.

"Discretion. You can fuck lover-boy all you want, but no more public displays of affection like tonight. No one knows except me and those closest to us," he says.

I frown, not wanting to agree. *How am I supposed to live a life where I keep the man I love hidden?*

"Love him; marry me. Love him in the shadows; pretend with me in the light."

I step between Lennox and the window, demanding his full attention. He doesn't back down, so I don't either.

He takes another step, forcing me to retreat until the back of my head hits the slanted glass of the window, and I have to stop. I comb my hand through my hair at the mistake I made moving in front of him with no escape route.

His arms come down on either side of my head, boxing me in. His tattoos creep out beneath his blue suit. His hair flops to one side as he throws me the serious stare he gives everyone. He uses it when he wants to pretend there will be hell to pay for disobedience.

I should fear a man like Lennox. He seems to have very little to lose and is willing to push the envelope of his morals to get what he wants. He cares about a handful of people, but I can't use any of those people against him.

Unfortunately, I care about the same people, and he knows that. He knows that he has me, and he can do whatever he wants with me. He may not physically touch me, but he can make my life hell if he wants to. He can control me. He can always change his mind about the rape thing too. He wouldn't be the first man in my life to make promises and then break them.

I won't back down. I can't just let him win, and I'm not afraid of him.

My heart beats up into my throat as he towers over me, and my defiance rises along with it.

He senses the change in me. Despite the progress he thinks he's made tonight, we are no further along in making an agreement than at the beginning of this meeting.

We both want what we want—he to become a Corsi boss, me to have my freedom. And neither of us can get what we want without the other.

The way he scowls at me tells me he knows it too. I'm what's standing in the way of getting what he wants, just as he is to me.

We're starting a dangerous game. That's all that's been decided tonight. One of us will win; one of us will lose. The stakes are high.

Who will land the first real blow?

I thought I did when I kissed Kit, but it was barely a surface scratch. I didn't wound Lennox—just annoyed him.

The crazed look in his eyes tells me he's about to land a bigger strike, though.

"You really love him?"

"Yes, of course. He's seen me through everything. He's my best friend."

"I don't think he is."

I frown. "Nothing you say is going to make me fuck you and give you heirs. If you want that, you'll have to take it from me."

"You want to bet?" he says with a sly smile, his eyes lighting up at the idea. I like his grin, even his conniving one, but I don't like the way it makes my body feel. I feel light-headed and weightless as an infusing warmth spreads through my body at his sexy grin.

"No, I don't want to bet. I know I love him. I have nothing to prove. I will never fuck you. You're giving me him but asking me to hurt the man I love. I can't do that."

"Why not? I will never rape you, only seduce you. It will always be your choice. If you love Kit so much, what do you have to lose?"

"You would never win a bet like that."

Lennox leans in until his breath is hot against my lips. His masculine scent overwhelms me, and I doubt I'll forget it soon.

I don't like it or his invasion of my space, but I refuse to yield and show him that.

His hand drops down, and his thumb rubs over my bottom lip. My tongue runs over the spot that his thumb just vacated.

He chuckles. "I think I have a decent shot. But if you really love Kit, if he's your person, then it won't be hard to resist me."

My nostrils flare, and if I knew how, I'd punch him right now and knock his smug expression off of his face. "What are the stakes?"

"If I win, we start trying for kids right away..." He pauses for dramatic effect. "And we do it the old-fashioned way. No IUI crap."

I frown, but it doesn't matter. There is no way I'm losing this bet. "And if I win, we don't try to have kids at all, and you never touch me except for a peck on the lips when we have to in public."

His eyes widen for a split second. He wasn't expecting that. I'm a Corsi—I'm expected to have heirs. It's my sole purpose in life as a woman in this world.

"If I seduce you, if I convince you to want me—a kiss, a touch, a fuck, *anything*—I win," he growls.

"And when I easily resist, then we don't have heirs, and I keep fucking Kit. If we must have kids, it will be *his* blood."

Lennox's throat tightens. "One year. If I can't seduce you by then, I'll give up."

"Deal."

I hold out my hand, and he takes it. Shaking my hand sends tiny jolts between us, almost forcing me to let go, but I just squeeze tighter, pushing through the shocking feeling.

Still holding my hand, he kneels down on one knee. Retrieving a box from his pocket, he pops it open and shoves it into my hands. "I don't lose, Rialta. If I were you, I'd give him up now before you break his heart even more."

I look down at the box in my hand to find an engagement ring. I expected something extravagant, something expensive meant to woo me.

Staring at it, my lips part involuntarily, and my heart thumps rapidly in my chest. It's a simple oval opal ring set in a rose gold band. It's elegant and unique and something I would have picked out for myself.

How would he know I hate diamonds? How would he know I prefer the creativity of a stone that seems to change colors depending on how you look at it?

"Opal represents a leap of faith, confidence in a relationship, and creativity. I thought you might like it more than a traditional diamond since you're an artist, and this relationship is going to take a leap of faith from both of us. But if you'd prefer a diamond, I'll exchange it for whatever you want."

I'm touched that he thinks I'm an artist. I assume Ri told him I liked to draw, and he's seen the tattoo I did on Beckett, but that's far from an artist.

"No...it's perfect," I murmur, stunned. My eyelids float up to Lennox.

He hesitates for a moment. I expect a simple, 'Rialta, will you marry me?' But Lennox is full of surprises.

Taking the ring box and my hands in his. He removes the ring and holds it out to me.

"Rialta, I know I'm not who you would choose. You're not in love with me. In fact, you're in love with another man. I doubt you will ever love me, and I can't promise I'll ever love you. I'm a cynical, overly protective grump who drives you crazy with my controlling nature and inability to relax and have fun. I rarely smile or laugh. I'm far too serious for my own good. But it makes me disciplined, a good fighter, and honorable.

"I don't know you that well—but I do know that life hasn't dealt you a fair hand. You drive me crazy with your childish antics and your impulsive, rebellious nature. I know you're creative, loyal, and protective of your family. I don't know if our marriage will last forever or if there will ever be love between us, but I do hope that someday we can grow to respect each other. I hope we can be loyal in the sense of not hurting each other intentionally. And I hope we can maybe learn to like each other through our shared interests." He takes a deep breath. "Rialta Corsi, will you do me the honor of marrying me?"

Lennox looks serious, as he almost always does, but

there's a softness in his gaze. His eyes hold a hope that we can make this work for us. He truly believes we can get married without killing each other and that it can be a mutual benefit to both of us.

He's right that he's not who I'd choose for myself. I'll never love him or ever think of him in the way a wife should think of her husband. But running away from him is not getting me anywhere. And fighting him, my father, and everyone else at every turn is childish and going to get someone killed.

I swallow hard and say the word that surprises us both, "Yes."

CHAPTER 6

Lennox

MY EYEBROWS RAISE in shock at her answer, but I quickly lower them. It won't help our relationship to be surprised when she does what I want instead of the snarky comment I expect.

Slipping it onto her finger, the ring fits perfectly.

"River knows?" she asks.

"I asked her opinion when I picked out the ring. She was also helpful with sizing."

She nods, staring down at it again. "I should be going now that the most important parts of our arrangement are settled."

I frown as I stand up. "Go? We barely have an agreement. We don't have anything in writing. We—"

"I just agreed to marry you. That's more than enough for tonight."

I snap my mouth shut. She's right—I should pick my battles, and tonight I won. Although, I would marry her tonight if she would allow it. Now that she's agreed, I don't want to give her a chance to back out.

"It's late. I'll help you find what you need upstairs in the bedroom, and I'll sleep on the couch," I say. Before she has a chance to protest, I jog up the black metal staircase to my bedroom in the loft.

I quickly pull out a fresh towel, toothbrush, shirt, and pair of shorts and set them all on the bathroom counter. Walking back into my bedroom, I scan it quickly. I recently changed the sheets, and I keep a tidy house, so she shouldn't have anything to complain about or uncover any secrets from sleeping up here alone.

When I turn around, she's already standing at the top of the stairs, looking at my dark grey queen-sized bed.

"You should find everything you need in the bathroom."

She nods, meeting my gaze with unnerving calm. "I'm sure I will."

There's a lump in my throat as I watch her step into the bathroom and shut the door. She's making this too easy.

Did she have a change of heart? Or is she planning to murder me in my sleep?

I jog down the stairs, texting Hayes and Gage with an update. I barely make it downstairs when the annoying, spoiled princess I'm used to returns.

Thumping music blares from my bedroom, rattling the walls and furniture. It's after midnight, so I'll definitely be getting an earful from my neighbors for this.

Groaning, I sprint back upstairs. I can't believe I need to scold my soon-to-be wife like a damn child.

"Rialta," I shout through the door, rapping my knuckles against the door.

The music gets louder, as does her voice singing along with the obnoxious tune.

"Rialta!" I try again.

She still doesn't answer me.

I grab the doorknob and shove my shoulder hard against the door, surprised to find she didn't bother locking it.

When I open the door, she's in nothing but her black bra and thong with the toothbrush hanging from her mouth. Her now-brushed hair cascades around her in long waves as she sings and shakes her ass in my tiny bathroom.

"What are you doing?" I ask, even though it's obvious. She's driving me insane.

"Getting ready for bed," she calmly answers in between lyrics.

"You're waking up the entire apartment building!" I shout over the sound of the music.

"What?"

"I said..." I sigh and grab her phone, turning the music off. My Bluetooth speakers finally give my ears a respite.

"Don't touch my stuff!" She yells, reaching for the phone back.

"Then stop being so inconsiderate."

She rolls her eyes and snatches the phone back from me. "This is who I am. I like music. I like singing. I like dancing. I like having fun. I like living. If you can't handle that, then too bad. It's not my fault you can only deal with dark and gloomy shit like this boring ass apartment."

My hands fist by my sides, and I see red. My doctor needs to put me on some blood pressure meds to deal with this chick embedded in my life and personal space.

"We need to find a different place to live once we get married. We won't survive here," I say.

"No, we don't need a different place."

"No? You just said you hated my dark, gloomy, *boring* apartment."

"No, I said an apartment like this is all you can handle. I didn't say that I didn't like it. I do."

"It's too small."

She resumes her music and ass shaking, and I can't help but stare. Her boobs bob up and down in her bra as her hips sway along with the music. *Why does she have to be so damn attractive?*

It would be easier if she were ugly. She's going to drive me crazy, and I won't be able to release my frustrations by fucking her hard against every surface in my apartment.

I reach onto the counter and pause her music again.

"It seems plenty big enough to me," she says.

I frown as a vein pops on my forehead, which makes her laugh.

"Calm down, Grandpa; you're going to give yourself a stroke."

"You do realize we're the same age, right? Stop calling me Grandpa."

"Stop acting like one," she shrugs.

"You mean stop acting responsibly?"

She shrugs again, finishes brushing her teeth, and then spits into the sink. My eyes are transfixed on her mouth the entire time, and I wonder what it would be like to taste her lips.

No, stop it. You already know what she would taste like —mint toothpaste and my dignity. I just haven't been laid in a long time. I would remedy that if it wouldn't cause more problems, but unfortunately, it would. I'm destined to remain celibate for a bit longer.

She turns the music back on, this time at a much softer volume and only emanating from her phone. Smiling, she slips on my shirt and shorts.

"Goodnight, Lennox." Her eyes twinkle with tortuous revenge. She thinks she regained some sliver of power after agreeing to marry me.

Her hips sway as she brushes past me and climbs into my bed.

I shake my head. "Goodnight, pain in my ass."

I turn and head back downstairs to my waiting couch.

Thank goodness the couch is big and comfy instead of small and stylish.

I undress to my boxer briefs and lay down on the couch, pulling a throw blanket over myself.

Her soft music still drifts down to where I'm trying to sleep, but at least it's not pissing off the neighbors.

I sigh and roll over, trying to drown out the music with one of the couch cushions. I'm going to need my sleep to deal with whatever antics she has planned for me next. She may have agreed to marry me, but she's made it clear she won't make it easy for me. If it's what I need to do to fix my problems, then I'll be ready for whatever she throws at me next.

CHAPTER 7

Rialta

STOPPING MY MUSIC, it quickly becomes too quiet as I lay in Lennox's bed. My heart is beating gently, my breathing is slow and calm, and my eyes keep fluttering shut. Lennox's bed is the most comfortable thing I've ever slept in. I swear it must be made of clouds or something.

But it's not just how it feels—it smells like him. It has his clean, sharp scent. It's a calming, protective smell that lulls me into a false sense of security.

I have the urge to turn my music back on as loud as I can to drown out the silence, but I've annoyed Lennox enough.

I replay every word of our conversation tonight, trying to understand him, but Lennox is an enigma. He's cold, serious, and unfeeling, but several times he showed me a softer, caring side too. And he gave me as much freedom as he could. He gave me Kit. He gave me the ability to have a say in what our marriage will be. He gave me the choice of where I want to live. He promised he would never force himself on me. And most importantly—our bet. He gave me the ability to decide if I ever fuck him, if I ever have his children. He gave me a lot, more than I could possibly have ever expected but not nearly enough all at the same time.

I will still be forced to marry him. Still forced to pretend. Still paraded around. Still expected to play the happy wife. Still told to hide Kit. Still blackmailed into hiding my true feelings, my real love, my true self.

My future doesn't feel like my own, and I'm still crushed by the weight of others' demands.

Lennox showed me he can be a good man, albeit an insufferable one. *But is that enough?*

I need to see Kit. He'll help me get some clarity.

I pull out my phone and text him Lennox's address. He texts back immediately, saying he'll be here in fifteen minutes to pick me up.

My heart races, and adrenaline fills my veins. This is what I'm used to feeling—a rush of danger and excitement. I have no idea what to do with this calm, safe feeling in Lennox's bed.

I get out of bed and search through Lennox's dresser for a sweatshirt. I find one and pull it over his T-shirt I'm wearing, but I don't see suitable shoes anywhere. The only shoes I have are my high heels, and Lennox's shoes are far too big.

I sigh—I guess I'm going barefoot.

I creep down the stairs, trying to decide if I should tell Lennox what I'm doing or not. He did say I could keep Kit. I can love Kit; I just have to marry Lennox. Even though it's after two in the morning, Lennox has nothing to be upset about.

Plus, if I wake him, Lennox will just insist on coming with me to keep me safe. And after the last encounter between them, I don't want Lennox to try to kill Kit again. Even if Lennox has agreed to let me keep Kit, I'm not sure I believe him yet. I'm not sure I believe any of it.

When I reach the first floor, I look over at Lennox on the couch. He's sound asleep with a pillow shoved over his ear.

I smile at how ridiculous he looks and decide against waking him. My grumpy future husband needs sleep, and I can sneak out and back in before he gets up.

I slip out the door, carefully closing it behind me. I expect to find Hayes or Gage keeping guard in the hallway, but I find it empty.

Hmmm.

I look around for cameras, assuming one of them is watching.

"I'll be right back. I'll be safe. I'm just going to see Kit, and Lennox is okay with it," I whisper to what I think is a camera in the corner of the hallway.

I wait a second to see if one of them is going to burst out from a nearby door and try to prevent me from leaving, but nothing happens.

I grin and head to the elevator banks. I'm downstairs in less than five minutes from when I texted Kit, so I don't expect him to be outside yet. But as I reach the lobby, his Corvette pulls up outside, and my smile reaches my eyes.

I chew my bottom lip, trying to hide my excitement as I run out. The second I take a step out of the building, rain pelts down on me, and my bare feet become instantly cold and wet. I don't care, though—I just need Kit right now.

I jump into the passenger seat of his car with childish glee. Before I can even say anything, Kit pulls me to him and kisses me aggressively.

I melt into his hold and allow his kisses to warm my chilled body. I don't know what I'm going to do about Lennox, but I do know that letting me keep Kit is the greatest gift he could give me. I don't know how I'm going to love him in the shadows, though. I don't know how I'm going to contain and cover up my love for him.

My heart overwhelms me, and tears start welling in my eyes. I shiver, trying to shake the hurricane of hot and cold in my head and body.

"Baby, are you okay? You're shivering. And are you crying?" Kit asks with concern.

"Some of the rain got in my eyes," I lie as I wipe my eyes on the sleeves of Lennox's sweatshirt. "I'm fine."

Kit frowns. "You're not fine. You're being forced to marry a man you hate. That's not fine."

I stroke Kit's smooth face and stare into his green eyes. They're full of sadness at seeing me lose myself. Kit is the opposite of Lennox in every way. He's sunshine, fun, and excitement. He exonerates his youth. His hair is short and light, while Lennox's unkempt locks are dark. Kit's skin is unmarked, while Lennox's is covered in tattoos. Kit has an honest job as a sales associate, while Lennox is an aspiring mob boss. Kit is an angel, and Lennox is the devil. Kit has my heart; Lennox my hate.

"We could run away. I have a passport and plenty of money saved. Let's start a new life somewhere else," he says with hope in his eyes, even though he's asked me a million times.

I shake my head. "We can't. They would find us. There's nowhere we could go that they wouldn't find us." *Plus, I wouldn't do that to River or Vincent. Despite everything that's happened, I love them both and don't want to abandon them.*

Kit sighs. "Then where to for tonight?"

I grip the back of his neck, stroke his face, and pull him into another kiss. "Somewhere where I can pretend we're back in Mississippi, sneaking out of our parents' houses and making out under the stars."

Kit's eyes twinkle with delight. "I can do that. Your fiancé won't be following us and trying to kill me again?"

"No, Lennox won't try to kill you anymore, I promise."

We have a lot to talk about, but first, I need to feel like a normal twenty-one-year-old. I at least need to pretend I have my whole future ahead of me and can date and marry anyone I want.

Kit zips away, driving quickly as I roll down my window to feel the breeze in my hair. It's not the same as driving through the countryside, but the city is relatively quiet. If I close my eyes, it's not hard to pretend we're out in nature instead of in the middle of a busy city.

The car stops, and I open my eyes to find Kit staring back at me with a flicker of desire in his eyes.

"I want you so badly, baby. Especially after last time was so abruptly interrupted."

"Then you should have me." I unbuckle my seatbelt and start to crawl across the center divider toward him.

He frowns. "Only for tonight. Your asshole future husband won't allow me to see you much longer without threatening to kill me again." He tilts my head back, and I see glaring red mixed with moisture in his eyes. "I gave you up once. I can't lose you again," he whispers.

I feel his heartache as I climb onto his lap. Straddling him and hovering my lips over his, I run my hands over his hair and down his neck. Kit peels off my sweatshirt, leaving me in my thin T-shirt to keep my body hidden from any onlookers.

There was once a time I was willing to be the perfect, obedient daughter. I was willing to give up the life I had built for myself and marry Beckett, the man my father chose for me. But like Beckett found a way to choose his own spouse, I'm not ready to give up my hope yet, either.

"You won't lose me again..." I kiss him softly, sucking his bottom lip into my mouth. He groans, and it vibrates his body.

"You can have me forever," I whisper into his ear.

He grabs my head and tilts me back again. "What do you mean? Did your father change his mind? Did Lennox? You don't have to marry him?"

My lips thin, and my heart beats rapidly for Kit. I wish I could take away all the pain he's going to have to endure watching me with another man. I still have hope I'll find a way out of having to marry Lennox, but I can't give Kit that hope.

He needs to prepare his heart and decide if he still wants to be with me, even if it's a half-life of a relationship. All I can offer him is sneaking around under the moonlight and fleeting moments together like this.

"No, I still have to marry Lennox on Saturday."

"Oh," he deflates.

I rub my thumb across his lips. "I hate even asking this of you because you deserve so much better, but I'm selfish."

He takes my hands in his and kisses them, his eyes full of love and want for me.

"I love you, bug. I would do anything for you."

"I love you, too." I take a deep breath. "He'll let me keep you."

"Lennox will let you keep me?" He says the words carefully, unsure of whether or not he heard me correctly.

I nod. "My marriage with Lennox would be a contract, a business arrangement. It wouldn't be a real marriage. I wouldn't have to fuck him. And he agreed that I could keep seeing you discreetly on the side."

"He agreed to let me be with the woman I love—how chivalrous of him," Kit says furiously. "He doesn't love you. He doesn't care about you. All he wants is to be the next don. And I don't believe he won't want to have sex with you. He's a dangerous man who wants power above all else. When it comes down to it, he'll expect you to fuck him. And if you refuse, he'll take what he wants from you."

I look down, feeling as furious as he is but not sure how to fix this. I agree with a lot of what Kit's saying, but I don't think Lennox will hurt me. I believed Lennox when he spoke, but there is no use telling Kit that. Only time will tell who's right and who's wrong.

Kit tilts my chin up, looking at me with watery eyes. "You don't have to do this. You don't have to marry him. We can find another way."

He keeps the tears within his eyes, but I don't.

My cheeks are flooded as I shake my head. "There isn't another way. This is the only way I get to keep you. It's not fair, and you deserve better—"

"No."

My heart stops. *Is he letting me go?* I don't know how I'll stand to stay married to Lennox if I don't have Kit, my best friend for all these years. It used to be River, but after spending so much of our lives apart, Kit is the only true friend I have left. It's why I was hesitant to ever become more than just friends with him—I've always been terrified of losing him.

"No, it isn't fair. But not having you in my life isn't an option. If this is truly the only way I get to keep you, then I'll take every moment I can get with you. And I won't have any regrets. I get to experience true love, and that's worth any cost, even if it means never getting to be your husband."

I kiss him.

It's not enough to show how much I love him. It's not enough at all.

Our lips devour each other in the front seat of his car. His hands grip my waist as mine grab his neck, and we both push our tongues deeper. He tastes like hope, freedom, and love. I don't think I even realized how much I love him until this moment, until he said how much he'd give up for me.

Now I know for sure that what I feel for him is love.

"I need you inside me right now," I pant against his lips.

The car is tiny. There's hardly any room for me to straddle him—definitely not enough room to have sex, but neither of us care. We'll make it work. We need each other too much.

My hands fumble at his jeans, trying to get to him as quickly as possible. His hands move to my ass, shoving Lennox's shorts down just as I get Kit's cock free. Our mouths interlock as we kiss each other harder and harder, melding our bodies together.

I raise my hips just enough for him to slip inside, hitting my head on the ceiling of the car.

Kit notices and puts his hand on my head—he's always protecting me and taking care of me. Lennox could learn a lesson or two about what it truly means to take care of someone.

I push Lennox out of my head and fuck the man I love. He's the man I vow to always fight for, even if it's only in my head. I may have to marry Lennox, but that doesn't mean I'm giving up. It doesn't mean I'll accept my fate. Someday, I will find a way out and a way to marry Kit instead.

He fucks me hard and fast—both of us needing a release, a desperate attempt to push our heartbreak away.

"I'm so close. Are you close?" Kit grunts.

I'm not, but I don't want to ruin this moment. "Yes," I cry.

"Come with me," Kit moans.

I moan with him, faking my orgasm as Kit pours his inside me. As I hold his head tight against my chest, I don't even care that I didn't come. This is what I wanted—this closeness.

I look at Kit, and we both break out smiling and laughing. We will find a way through this together—I have no doubt about that.

But just as I start to believe we'll find a way out of my marriage with Lennox, the metal clink of a gun coming to rest against the car window shatters the illusion.

CHAPTER 8

Rialta

OUR EYES WIDEN with terror as we stare into the barrel of the gun outside the window. This time, it isn't Lennox on the other side of the window. I feel Kit slipping out of me, but neither of us dare move a muscle more. Kit has never had a gun held to his head before me. He's never known how dangerous my life truly is until this week, and I was reckless with him.

This was my mistake.

If he's going to be in my life, I have to protect him. Figuring out a better way to protect him will have to wait until another time, though—that is, if we live through this.

"Lower the window," the man snarls on the other side of the glass.

Kit is frozen; he doesn't move. I'm pretty sure he's in shock.

Anger trembles through me. I'm so stupid to think this was okay. How naive to think I should date anyone not in the mafia world. Kit isn't prepared to defend himself.

This situation isn't fair to Kit, but I don't know how I'm supposed to give him up either.

I slowly move my hand to the door and press the window button. Slowly, the glass lowers.

"Good girl," the man says condescendingly. "Now, don't move, or I'll kill you both."

Kit and I are frozen in our positions as the strange armed man reaches his hand in through the window, unlocks the car, and then opens the door.

"Get out, Princess."

My eyes peer into Kit's, trying to tell him to remain calm. Everything is going to be okay; I'll make sure of it.

But his eyes are unblinking blank discs. He's not in any state to understand what I'm trying to silently convey.

I slowly climb off of Kit and put my feet on the cold, wet ground. Rain is still pouring down, soaking my shirt. Lennox's shorts grow heavy with the water and fall to my ankles.

I peek back at Kit, knowing he's exposed and vulnerable.

"Don't hurt him, and I'll do whatever you want," I say fiercely.

The man still has the gun pointed at me, thankfully, and not Kit. He's wearing a dark ski mask and all-black clothes, so I can't make out who he is.

"You'll do what I say because I have a gun pointed at your head, Princess."

I roll my eyes. "I'm not a princess, and I'm not afraid of you."

"You're mafia royalty, so your father will pay handsomely for your return."

I narrow my eyes in confusion. I don't know who this man is yet, but the fact he's considering using me for ransom tells me a few things. He must not be the one that keeps trying to kill every member of my family if he's only interested in cash.

"Turn around," he barks at me.

I do, taking a deep breath as the man grabs my arms and jerks them behind my body. He quickly ties them together with rough rope that scratches and digs into my skin.

Kit finally blinks as he sees what's happening.

"Go," I mouth at him.

He just stares at me in disbelief—either at the situation, how calm I am, or both.

"Go, now," I mouth more insistently.

A flash of lighting lights up the sky, and then a burst of thunder claps a second later. The sound must knock Kit out of his stupor because he finally puts his foot on the gas, and his Corvette takes off.

"Hey!" the man tying the rope shouts at him. But before the man can grab his gun, Kit is far enough away to avoid being shot.

I smile and blow out a breath. *Kit's safe; that's all that matters.*

The man finishes tightening the ropes on me as rain pours down my face harder now, making it hard to see more than a foot in front of my eyes. I'm surprisingly calm for being kidnapped.

This isn't the first time it's happened to me, and I've always survived. From the sound of it, I'll survive this time too. But that doesn't mean I won't end up hurt, raped, or violated.

The man jerks on my arms, pulling me backward. "Get in the van."

I feel the cold metal of the gun on the side of my head again.

I blink, trying to make out where said van is, but there's water in my eyes, and I can't see anything.

He yanks my arms hard and then shoves me from behind.

I stumble, my shins hitting the bottom of the van. I fall

forward face first, landing hard on thinly carpeted floor hard inside the van.

I sigh as I hear the side door roll shut behind me, and the man gets into the front seat.

I should try to escape, try to break out of the rope, or come up with an escape plan at least. But I know it's useless. I have plenty of skills, but breaking out of rope bindings, escaping, fighting, using a gun—these aren't them.

I much prefer drawing, painting, sculpting—anything artistic. But right now, I'm regretting my decision not to learn basic self-defense. I'm a mafia princess. I'm not supposed to know self-defense. I'm supposed to look pretty and produce male heirs to carry on the Corsi line. It would be inappropriate for me to know how to defend myself and look poorly on Lennox if he wasn't able to do it himself.

This world is so stupid and sexist, but I also know it's deeper than that.

Vincent loves me. He loved me so much that he sent me away for my entire childhood to protect me. He never thought I was strong enough. He never thought I could learn to protect myself—that's the real reason I never learned. He's bucked enough mafia traditions; he would have no problem breaking this one too.

I'm the weak one. River was always the strong one. I'm the carefree one, as proven by how calm my heart rate currently is. I could die tonight, but if you took my blood pressure right now, you'd never know it. I guess that's my superpower: when the man who is after me finally catches me, and that gun or knife is aimed at my head, and I know the real end is near, I won't be afraid. My heart won't race. I'll die without fear.

I shake my head against the floorboard. It's not a very helpful strength to have because it won't save me. I'll still be dead.

The van roars and turns through the city streets while I contemplate my entire life.

Suddenly, the van comes to a screeching halt.

I hear the slice of a bullet through glass and flesh as the man in the front seat slumps over the wheel. A second later, more gunfire erupts all around me.

There must have been more men working with the ski mask guy, I realize.

The van door loudly slides open behind me.

I should be relieved, but I know how badly I fucked up. Whoever my rescuer is isn't going to be happy that I went off on my own without protection.

I'm pulled up into a sitting position and come face to face with River.

She exhales audibly, happy to see I'm alive and unhurt.

"Follow me," she says calmly. Holding her gun in front of herself and using her body to shield me, we head out into the rain.

Shots are still whizzing all around us, and I realize just how many more people are here.

"Fuck, Kit. He—"

"He's okay," River says, cutting me off curtly. We don't have time for conversation now.

I spot River and Beckett's SUV and follow River to one of the rear passenger doors. She flings it open, shoves me inside hard, and closes the door all before whipping around and firing her gun.

She's such a badass. She never needed a rescuer. She could always protect herself, unlike me.

I sigh as I keep my head down and don't move, knowing the drill.

A few minutes later, the front doors open, and Beckett and River climb into the front. Beckett steps on the gas, and we peel out without a word.

I open my mouth to speak but bite my tongue. I'm lying in the middle row with my hands still tied behind my back. There are a lot of words I could say, but none that seem right. I settle on, "Thank you."

River turns and looks at me with a soft smile. "Of course, Rialta. I'm just glad you're okay. But we need to talk tomorrow after everyone has gotten sleep. I want to understand what happened. Did Lennox kick you out and not offer to send his men to protect you? What happened?"

I shake my head. "No, this isn't Lennox's fault. I snuck out. It's my fault."

River's face drops in disappointment, but she quickly recovers. "I'm just glad you're safe, but you really have to be more careful. I don't know what I'd do without you."

"Same," I say.

I look up and meet Beckett's gaze in the rearview mirror. He's silent and stewing. He clearly has something he wants to get off his chest, but he won't say it in front of River.

The rest of the drive back to Lennox's apartment is silent. While the car is quiet, my mind is not. It's whirling with too many thoughts. Thoughts of how stupid I was. How selfish. How I risked so many lives. How Kit could have died because of me. How I should give him up. How I know that I can't. How I don't know how to solve any of my problems.

The car eventually stops.

"Wait in the car," Beckett tells River, gently leaning over and kissing her tenderly on the cheek.

She nods, which isn't like her. She doesn't like to be ordered around by Beckett, even for small things.

Beckett opens my door and pulls me out roughly before slamming the door shut behind me.

"I'm sorry," I say. He needs to hear me apologize, but I'm not exactly sure why.

"You have to grow up, Rialta. You can't keep doing this. You can't..." he trails off as the rain flicks down over his eyelashes and then down his face.

"I'm sorry, okay? I'm sorry! I never meant to risk Kit's life. I never meant to make you all worry. I never meant to make you get up in the middle of the night to come to rescue me. I never—"

"You don't think, Rialta!" His anger is palpable as he grabs onto my bicep, yanking me like he can somehow shake the carelessness out of me. He lets go and runs his hand through his hair.

"I'm sorry," I say again, softer this time and meaning it. I like to live without fear, but I never want to put others at risk in order for me to live my life.

"Sorry isn't good enough, not this time."

I narrow my eyes, trying to make out his expression through the rain.

"Ri's pregnant. I won't let her risk her life to protect you, not anymore. It's our child's life she's risking every time she has to save your selfish ass," Beckett says.

My mouth falls open. I'm so happy for them but feel so incredibly stupid. I would have never risked their future baby's life for mine. *Never.*

Before I can respond, Beckett is climbing back in the SUV and driving off. When I turn back toward the apartment building, Lennox is standing there, watching with as much disappointment on his face as I feel.

Fuck.

CHAPTER 9

Lennox

FROM THE SHADOWS of the apartment building's awning, I listen to Beckett confirm what I already knew to be true—Ri is pregnant. I watch shock spread across Rialta's face.

So she didn't know. I figured Ri would have told her. I guess that makes me forgive Rialta a little for not knowingly putting Ri at risk, but only just a little. Rage is coursing through my veins still, and it's taking everything inside me not to teach Rialta a lesson right here.

I love Ri like a sister. I want her to be happy, and she desperately wants a baby. It makes me irate that Rialta risked Ri's baby's life.

I force myself to take a deep breath to decrease the odds of me strangling Rialta. Then I make a mental note to throw a party to celebrate Ri and Beckett's baby when I get a chance.

Beckett finishes talking and then nods in my direction, as if saying she's my problem now. I watch him walk back to their SUV and take off.

He's right. Rialta is my problem now, and I won't let Ri

and Beckett be her sole protectors anymore. They have bigger things to worry about than babysitting a moody twenty-one-year-old who still acts like she's sixteen most of the time.

Rialta is yet to acknowledge my presence as I step out of the rain toward her. I grab her bicep and lead her into the apartment building. She's soaked, wearing nothing but one of my white T-shirts. The wet shirt is thin and entirely see-through now. She isn't wearing anything underneath—no bra or underwear. Her hair is dripping in wet cords, and her arms are tied behind her back.

As I wordlessly guide her to the stairs, I can't tell if she's crying or if it's the rain dripping off her black eyelashes.

"We aren't taking the elevator?" she asks.

"No," is the only answer I give her. I need time before being alone with her in my apartment. Otherwise, I'm likely to decide marrying her is a horrible decision and completely change my plan. Climbing the stairs will get out some of my frustration and give her time to contemplate her night's decisions.

She doesn't protest as we start up the stairs. We climb the flights in silence, and my frustration ever so slightly eases.

When we make it upstairs, Gage and Hayes are waiting in the hallway with worried faces.

"Lennox, we—" Hayes starts.

"Not now. You two fucked up, and I'll deal with you later," I snap. It's the first time I've ever bossed them around. Even though we're all the same age, I've always felt like the older brother. I've always taken the blame for their actions, always cleaned up their messes.

I'm tired of it.

Gage opens his mouth to object, but he immediately shuts it when steam comes out of my nostrils, and the vein pops on my forehead. I push Rialta into my apartment and slam the door shut.

Rialta's shoulders rise and fall sharply as she stands in the living room of my apartment, once again staring out the window into the night. I don't know what time it is, just that it's late.

I was such a fool for thinking we had made progress tonight. Of course, she would run off instead of doing the compliant thing—staying the fuck in my apartment.

Rialta turns and faces me. Water is dripping off her down onto my rug. She looks like a sad, wet puppy about to be scolded. She is right about one thing—I intend to teach her a lesson.

"Are you going to untie me?" she asks.

"No," I answer, even though I suspect she already guessed that. "You got yourself into this mess; you can get yourself out."

"I didn't intend to get held at gunpoint, to get tied up, and almost get kidnapped. I didn't think anyone would be after me tonight. I—"

"Didn't you listen to anything I said earlier? I'm fucking tired of you not thinking."

She narrows her eyes at me. "Isn't it your job to keep me safe? What if I had been kidnapped from my room? You and your men wouldn't have been prepared, so why should I trust you?"

"Why should I trust *you*, when you don't tell me you're leaving? You snuck out to see another man in the middle of the night."

"Kit isn't just some man; he's the love of my life. And if you don't want to deal with me anymore, I'd be happy to leave and go marry him."

"And you'd be dead within the week."

"At least I'd spend my last week happy. With you, I'll just be miserable, that is, if you can even keep me safe."

I take a step toward her. Her eyes widen, and her mouth closes. She's a spitfire, a hellraiser, a confident woman unafraid of anyone. She thinks she's weak because she doesn't know how to hold a gun or throw a punch, but she's much stronger than she thinks she is. She wouldn't have survived this long otherwise.

For her safety, I'm not sure if I should show her how strong she is or break her to make her feel weak. The latter state is definitely easier for me to protect. If she realizes her strength, she'll become even more brazen and an even bigger pain in my ass.

I wish I could say protecting her is because I care about her. While I'm not a completely heartless man, keeping Rialta alive and happy has little to do with her and all to do with my end goal. I can only accomplish my mission if I marry Rialta and she stays alive.

To help me decide, I test the waters to see how she'll react to my touch. I reach my hand out, touching the side of her cheek and then slowly running it down her neck to her exposed clavicle.

She shivers. "What are you doing?"

I continue running my hand down her body, down her arms, down the curves of her side until my hand reaches the hem of my shirt she's wearing, barely above her ass.

I wait to see her tremble in fear.

I wait to hear her tell me to stop.

Instead, she looks at me more defiantly. *Show her how strong she is it is.*

I stare at her with lust-filled eyes as I let my hand run down her thigh. It isn't hard to show attraction to her—she's a beautiful woman.

What I don't expect is the glint of longing in her eyes.

No matter how hard she tries to deny it, she's attracted to me almost as much as she loathes me. She may think she's in love with Kit, but she can't be if she reacts this easily to my gaze. Someday she'll realize that.

I shove my shirt up her thigh, feeling her ice-cold skin heat beneath my touch. I drag my hand up her thigh and over her hip, teasing her with where my hand might slip to next.

"What are you doing?" she tries again.

"Do you know how easy it would have been for those men to touch you?"

She grinds her teeth together. "I don't need you to tell me."

"I think I do." I slide my hand over her bare ass. She stiffens but still doesn't tell me to stop. "You don't understand what was at stake when you left my apartment."

"I understand. I don't need you mansplaining anything to me."

I pull her to me, feeling her chilled body flush against mine. She has to crane her neck to look up at me. My hand continues slinking up her body, over the dip at her waist, and up to the swell of her breast.

She sucks in a breath.

"When you left here without telling anyone, without taking security, without telling *me*—you put your life at risk." I reach for her silky wet hair. "I could be cleaning up your brains off the street."

She swallows hard.

"You could have been taken, locked in a dungy basement without any food, left to starve." I run my hand over her bare stomach. "Do you know what it's like to be hungry, Princess? I doubt you do. You wouldn't like it."

Her eyes swell, but she still doesn't fight back.

"You could be tied to a bed with a man twice your age

thrusting inside you. He wouldn't care if he made you bleed. He wouldn't care if you'd be haunted by him for the rest of your days. He wouldn't care how he hurts you.

"And oh, how he would hurt you. He'd defile you; make you wish you were dead instead of having to deal with the unending pain. Even if we were to rescue you, you wouldn't ever escape the nightmares, not really. You'd heal—but never fully. You'd carry that with you forever. Is that what you want?"

I let my hand hover over the slit between her legs. For a second, I want to touch her. I want to make her feel good and forget about all the pain she's caused me. For a second, I don't see her as the naive young woman who doesn't truly understand the risks of this dark world. Instead, I only see the sexy woman tied up in front of me and feel desperate to fuck her.

She shifts, and my hand rests between her legs, feeling the warmth of fire there.

My eyes widen at the realization that I'm not in control at all. Rialta may have her arms tied behind her back and be wearing nothing but my soaked shirt, but she won't go down without a fight. She called my bluff.

I won't rape her. I won't take anything from her. And yet, I don't move my hand away.

"You think I don't know what I risked?" Her eyes light up as she speaks.

"I don't think you have a clue what you could have lost. You've lived in your seaside mansion with your perfect adopted parents, private school, and preppy clothes. You expected to go to college, find a wealthy husband, and spend your life traveling—living your cozy little life. You never thought you'd have to return to this world. When you left, you were a child. You didn't understand the risks then, and you still don't now. This is the world we live in. We are all one second away from torture, rape, and death."

"You don't know anything about me," she barks back.

"I do. I know everything that's important. If you don't change your behavior, you're going to be the death of us all."

She shakes her head. "I didn't live in a cushy mansion. I didn't have rich adoptive parents. I didn't attend a preppy school. I lived in a tiny two-bedroom house. I've known what it's like to go hungry more times than not. I know what it's like to be touched by a man against my will. I've worked every day after school since I was thirteen, hoping to have enough money to feed and clothe myself.

"My adoptive mother was nice, but she worked three jobs and was never around. My adoptive father makes Vincent look like an angel. Vincent had no choice but to let me grow up this way. He couldn't send money if he wanted to keep me hidden. He hid me with a poor family in the middle of Mississippi, knowing I wouldn't have the best childhood, but I would survive. Living that way made me a survivor; it made me strong."

Her eyes flick back and forth over mine, surprised at herself by telling me her story.

"I've always known my life is at risk. I've always known I could be raped, tortured, or kidnapped again. My life is fleeting, and I'll be lucky if I see thirty years on this earth. I don't need you to tell me." The fury in her voice vibrates between her and me. Clearly, I've judged her wrong.

"I can't protect myself. You can lock me in a cage and throw away the key so no one can hurt me, but that's not a life. That's not what I want. I want to *live* whatever life I have left."

I hear the truth in every word, and I finally hear her. I finally understand her.

"But I don't want to risk innocent lives, especially not

River's baby. I don't want to risk Kit. So you don't have to worry about me running off without security again."

I watch her closely, but I believe every word she says. Call me naive, but apparently, her weakness is caring too much about others and not enough about herself. I know how that feels.

"For the record, I did announce my intentions to the hallway security camera. I assumed Hayes and Gage were watching. But in the future, I'll make sure I have protection with me, and you know exactly where I'm going."

I nod, not sure what else to say.

"I'm not the selfish, spoiled brat you think I am. I'm not an asshole like you, Lennox. I'm just a woman trying her best to live with what little life she has left without hurting anyone she loves in the process."

She licks her lips. "Stop playing games with me. Remove your hands from my body, and never touch me again without my expressed permission. And then untie me. *Now.*"

I remove my hand and take a step back, then pull a knife from my pocket. Slowly, I walk behind her and slice through the rope that has rubbed her skin raw.

I want to scoop her in my arms, carry her upstairs, and bandage her wounds. But I know that's not what she wants. It's the part of me that cares too much about other people begging me to take care of her. It wouldn't matter who is standing in front of me—if I see someone hurt, I want to fix it.

I frown, hating the way I am. I hate the burden I carry and how ill-tempered it makes me.

She doesn't seem to notice my inner conflict as she wordlessly heads upstairs, leaving me with more questions and confusion about who Rialta Corsi really is and how I'm going to marry her without ending up dead in the process.

CHAPTER 10

Rialta

THREE DAYS until I get married. I thought I'd feel more anxious the closer we get to the day, but after talking to Lennox, after what happened with Kit, I realized it's better if I stop fighting and just accept this situation. In the span of one night, I've gone through all of the stages of grief and landed at acceptance. I've accepted my fate. I still have hope for the future, but for now, I'm to be married to a man I hate. But he's also a man who has given me more freedom than I expected to get.

For now, my only job is keeping everyone I love safe. And that starts now.

Lennox and I wait in the lobby of his apartment, as we watch Beckett pull his Escalade in front of the building. Lennox hasn't spoken to me all morning, and I haven't spoken to him. We both said and did a lot of things last night that we have to be sorry for, but voicing the apology won't change anything.

Lennox walks out, and to my surprise, holds the rear passenger door open for me.

I give him a slight nod of acknowledgment, but before I

climb in, I have to do something. I move around him and open the passenger door, where River is sitting.

"I'm sorry. I should have never risked your life like that." Tears well in my eyes. "But I'm so, so happy for you."

Moisture builds in River's eyes as she breaks out into a big smile. "I wanted to tell you, but I didn't want you to fire me as your security team when you still clearly need me. And you have nothing to be sorry for."

I wrap my arms around her, and she squeezes me tight.

"Well, I hate to break it to you, but you are starting your maternity leave early if you won't quit outright," I say.

River glares at me.

"Lennox and the guys can protect me." I put my hand on the small curve of her stomach, only just beginning to show what is hidden beneath. "You have to protect my niece or nephew."

Tears fall down her cheeks, but she nods her head.

"We need to go, or we're going to be late," Beckett says from the driver's seat.

I nod and wipe my own eyes.

And then I climb in the backseat where Lennox is still holding the door open for me. He shuts it and walks around to the other side, giving a quick congratulations to River as well before climbing into the backseat next to me.

The car is silent as Beckett drives toward Vincent's condo. We are all thinking about what this meeting is going to involve. As much as we are all Vincent's favorite people, it doesn't shield us from his temper or wrath. It won't stop him from killing one of us if we piss him off.

When we arrive, Beckett takes River's hand, while Lennox and I follow solemnly behind. One of Vincent's guards shows us to his office when we arrive, where he's already seated behind his grand desk. Four chairs have been arranged in a semi-circle facing him. We all take a seat without a word, waiting for Vincent to begin.

"I hear congratulations are in order," Vincent says.

"Thank you," River says as Vincent walks over and hugs her. The second he does, everyone is at ease. I don't know how he found out, but it reminds us that we are all the family the man has. River—his adopted daughter. Beckett—his son-in-law. Me—his daughter. And Lennox—his soon-to-be-son-in-law and future successor. We are all the man has.

They take their seats again, and then Vincent starts again. "I wanted to speak to you about the wedding and ensure everything is in order. We're only a few days away."

"Three days," I say under my breath. *Three days, two hours, and twenty minutes to be exact.* I could probably count down to the exact second if asked.

Everyone's eyes go to me, but when I don't say more, Vincent continues. "River, you are in charge of getting the decorations, dresses, tuxes, et cetera, in order. The wedding will be at Holy Name Cathedral, which I've already booked. And the reception will be at The Langham. Spend as much money as necessary."

"Already on it. I have most of the decorations planned, and the tuxes are already ordered. And I plan on taking Rialta dress shopping this afternoon."

I suck in a breath at River's words and glance over at Lennox, who seems unfazed by the talk of the wedding planning. It doesn't bother him at all. Honestly, I could care less what dress I wear, or what the decorations are, or what the cake flavor is. None of it matters. The only wedding I will ever care about is to a man I love, and Lennox doesn't fit the bill.

"Beckett, you are in charge of security. Ensure your men

are prepared for any scenario, and I will give you a list of the men I trust most."

"Of course," Beckett answers.

"Rialta..." Vincent starts but stops, then clears his throat, his voice turning harsh. "Give him up."

I frown, but I know who *him* is. Give Kit up. I side-eye Lennox out of the corner of my eye, assuming he ratted me out, but he's frowning, too, as if he doesn't like this news any more than I do. *Interesting.*

"And Lennox, does our deal still remain? Are you prepared to take the blood oath on Saturday?"

"Yes," Lennox replies sternly.

All of our eyes turn to him, trying to read between the lines of what the blood oath is and what deal he's made. I assume it has to do with protecting me and being loyal to the Corsi line, renouncing his connection to the Retribution Kings. Otherwise, he'll become Vincent's greatest enemy. But staring at Lennox, something tells me it's more than that. He's trying to show no emotion, but I see the way his jaw tightens, his body stiffens, and his nostrils flare ever so slightly.

"Good, then you all have your orders. I'll see you all on Saturday," Vincent says, dismissing us.

Lennox gets up and walks out of the room swiftly, and I chase after him. River and Beckett stay behind. I can faintly hear her discussing details of the wedding planning with Vincent as I leave the room. They're most likely giving me some privacy to talk to Lennox.

Lennox makes it to the elevator before I do, and the doors nearly close before I put my hand in to stop them.

Panting heavily, I step inside, and the doors close immediately behind me.

Lennox looks straight ahead. He pretends not to notice

me or be watching some invisible movie playing before his eyes.

"Will you talk to me? Tell me what deal you made with my father." I don't know why I need to know, just that I do. Call it a gut feeling.

"No."

I frown. "Why not?"

"Because it's none of your concern."

"Except, it is. It's my life we're talking about! I deserve to know. What are you expected to do in exchange for marrying me and becoming my father's heir?"

The doors open on the ground floor, and Lennox starts to step out but then stops, standing between the doors as he turns and looks back at me.

What are you up to, Lennox? And how do I beat you?

"Fine, don't tell me. But I'm not giving up Kit, no matter what you or my father says," I say.

"I'm not telling you to give him up. Keep Kit around as long as you want. Hurt him all you want. I don't care." He leans in close, his mouth hovering over my ear as he steps back into the elevator, abruptly invading my space. His breath is hot on my neck as he says, "But know that before our year together is up, you'll be in my bed begging me to fuck you. And Kit will be nothing but a fleeting memory— an ex who couldn't live up to the real deal."

Then Lennox slams his hand between the closing elevator doors, catching them at the last minute, and steps out. I'm left gaping, hot and bothered, and completely confused about this enigma of a man and why I'm soaked between my legs.

CHAPTER 11

Lennox

TWO DAYS. Only two more days until I'm married. Two days until I either make the best or worst decision of my life.

I open the door into Hayes and Gage's apartment. They're more social than me, enjoying living together, while I can't stand sharing my space with anyone. I guess that's about to change in two days. I cringe at that thought.

Their apartment is bigger than mine—two actual bedrooms, one shared bathroom, an open floorplan living and kitchen area, and a dining room converted into an office. Gage is in the makeshift office, sitting behind a dozen monitors at a large desk.

He turns in his chair when he hears me approach. Hayes takes a seat in a nearby chair next to Gage.

"Tell me you've dug up something on Kit Taylor," I say, falling into one of the chairs.

"Kit grew up in Mississippi in foster care with very little money. He's been best friends with Rialta since Corsi sent her away. They grew up next door to each other. He had the same foster parents from the time he was five, but they never adopted him. No evidence of abuse, but they didn't have a lot of money. He graduated high school with decent grades but never attended college. Despite that, he's done quite well for himself. He works for a sales firm, where he makes a great commission, but it seems like he spends all of his money on a flashy car and bachelor pad."

"Is he a threat?" I ask.

"No, he's just an ordinary guy. He knows very little of Rialta's real life, except that she's being forced into an arranged marriage and that her father is a dangerous man. I'm not even sure Kit realizes he's mafia," Hayes says.

Dammit, I really wanted an excuse to kill him. Maybe if I'm lucky, I'll find a reason eventually.

I stare off into space, contemplating a plan of how this is going to work.

Gage takes one look at me and knows that I'm rethinking everything. "Stick to the plan, Lennox. This will work. It has to."

"I know. It will work. I had to change tactics slightly, but I know that it will."

"What do you mean?"

I sigh, not having told them all of the details of the deal I made with Corsi yet, knowing they might try to talk me out of it if I told them how serious it is if I lose. But we are in this together, and they deserve to know.

"Vincent Corsi wants me to find the man who has been hunting them for years. The man responsible for his children's and wife's death. He's been searching for them for years, but he won't name me as his successor until I find him."

Hayes frowns. "That's a tall order, even for us."

I nod.

"What tactic did you change? How are you going to let him name you as head of the Corsi mafia?" Gage asks.

"He told me to fall in love with Rialta. He said if I loved

her, then he could trust that she was as safe as if the man who wants to kill her was dead."

"I can understand that," Gage says.

"Yes, but I'll never fall in love with her. So you can see my conundrum. I can't do either, but I have to become the next Corsi boss."

Gage sighs. "So what are you going to do?"

"I'm going to make her fall in love with me."

Gage doesn't speak. I can tell from his expression he doesn't agree, but we all agreed to our parts of the plan. I'm in control of this part, and he won't argue as long as I uphold my end of the deal.

Hayes is biting his lip, and I know he won't hold back his thoughts much longer.

"If she falls in love with me, Vincent won't deny me. And it will make it easier for him to believe I love her in return, even if I don't."

"I see." Gage stares down at his computer.

"Well, you aren't exactly a ladies' man, but I can give you a few pointers. We'll have her falling in love with you in no time," Hayes says with his optimistic smile.

I nod. "You better get to teaching me quick."

Hayes frowns when I agree with him instead of giving a quick retort.

"Because if I fail, I'm a dead man."

Both of their eyes jump open, and I spend the rest of the night arguing with them, convincing them that our plan will still work. It has to work—for all of our sakes.

ONE DAY.

Only one day left until the wedding.

Everything is planned.

I picked out a dress with River.

Beckett has the security team assembled.

And Lennox hasn't decided to back out.

It's happening in one day.

I lay in a bed in River's apartment all day.

I don't get up to talk to her.

I don't get up for food.

I barely get up to use the bathroom.

Kit texts me, wanting to talk.

All I could text back was *I'm sorry.* But I forced myself to text more. *We can talk after. You can tell me if you still want to be with me. I love you.*

I turned off my phone after I texted. I didn't want to see his response.

I didn't want to see him promise he'd be with me no matter if I was married to another man, no matter the risk to his life.

Or if he told me he was done, and we're breaking up.
I'm numb.
I don't feel anything.
I don't think about Lennox.
I don't think about Kit.
I don't think about my future.
All I can think about is—one day.
I hear the clock ticking—over and over and over.
Tick tock.
Tick tock.
Tick tock.
Time's almost up.

CHAPTER 13

Lennox

"BE READY FOR ANYTHING," I say to Hayes and Gage as we pull up to the church in our black tuxedos. We're always on guard for an attack, but today especially so.

They both nod solemnly. Even Hayes, who is usually chipper, has a serious expression on his face.

We get out of the car and walk toward the church as a unit. I'm getting married in an hour, and I haven't heard from Rialta. But the lack of communication makes me assume she's going to go through with this. I'm ready for anything, though, including her deciding to run instead of marrying me.

Hayes stops me just before we reach the church steps. "Are you sure?"

I look from him to Gage, who is also looking at me like he thinks this is a terrible idea. But we all have to take big risks to achieve our goals. I'm willing to die. And I know they would make the same decision.

"Yes," I say firmly, my tone directing them to never ask me again.

Hayes steps to the side, and we enter the church. The

sanctuary is beautiful. Large ceilings, stained glass windows, classic wooden pews, and marble floors. Ri decorated it with classic white flowers and candles—very romantic.

Too bad there is nothing romantic about today.

I still can't believe this is happening. I'm about to be a married man.

A few weeks ago, it was Beckett who was about to be married to Rialta. And now, it's me.

One of Vincent's men approaches us as we stand in the aisle of the sanctuary.

"Follow me," he says, not introducing himself or telling us where we are going.

But we all know—the blood oath.

I have no idea what it entails, what I'm expected to do, or what vows of loyalty I will have to make. But I do know what the Retribution Kings would expect, and it makes me want to run in the other direction. Whatever it is, I'm sure it will make saying my wedding vows feel like a piece of cake instead of the hell I know it's going to be.

We follow the guard through the sanctuary to a hallway at the back and then through a door that leads to a staircase and down to the church basement. We all have our hands inches from our guns, prepared for anything.

An unsettling feeling washes over me as I step into the basement and find Vincent Corsi standing in his tux in the center of the room, with a dozen of his closest men surrounding him.

If I don't take the oath, I won't be leaving this basement alive. Neither will Hayes or Gage.

I calm my emotions as I stand in the basement facing Corsi. Feel nothing, no fear, just pure determination. I know Gage and Hayes, standing at either side of me, are doing the same.

"Lennox Crane, you have been chosen to marry my

daughter, Rialta Corsi," Corsi starts, and the room goes absolutely silent.

I'm careful not to move or let my heart race. I will not let them think I'm afraid. I've faced death enough times that it barely phases me anymore. My only fear is that I won't complete my mission before I die.

"Today, you will say vows before her and God, but you will also say your vows before us," he continues.

I meet Corsi's eyes with determination. Nothing he says or tells me to do will make me back down. I must marry Rialta. I must become Corsi's successor.

"Lennox, do you vow today to give up your name? Give up who you once were and become a Corsi?"

"I do," I answer him. "I, Lennox Crane, will forevermore be known as Lennox Corsi."

He nods, satisfied with my answer. "Do you vow your loyalty to the Corsi name and to all who defend it?"

I look from Corsi to the others in the room. "I promise."

"Do you vow to give up your loyalty to the Retribution Kings?" He narrows his eyes at me, expecting this part to be the most difficult for me. I was raised as a Retribution King. It's all I've ever known—but it's not who I am.

He doesn't realize my history with them. It's complicated, and there's so much darkness associated with them that I've tried to put in the past.

I'll be glad in a way to start anew.

"I give up any loyalty I once had to the Retribution Kings. I am no longer a Retribution King. I am now a Corsi. I am one of you. And I'm proud to call you my new family."

Corsi looks at me with cruel eyes. He may love his daughters and treat them kinder than most dons, but this look is the man most of the world knows. He is pure cruelty.

"Then prove your loyalty in blood."

I hold my breath, knowing this is the painful part. I still

don't know what's expected of me, but the moment has arrived.

Corsi gives a nod, and his men part behind him. Two men drag a man forward. His arms are tied behind his back, a gag rests in his mouth, and his eyes are wild with fear.

In two seconds, I recognize him as a Retribution King. And I immediately know what is expected of me. I'll lose what's left of my soul if I do this.

I barely knew him, but he's only a couple of years older than me. I never heard a bad thing about him, but that doesn't mean he isn't a bad guy. I'm sure, like everyone else here, he's killed, but that doesn't mean he deserves to die. It doesn't mean he killed maliciously or killed innocent people. I know very little of his history, but he's never given me cause to want him dead.

And yet, he's a Retribution King. He knows every day could be his last. Death is always a possibility when you're in one of these gangs.

"Kill your fellow Retribution King. Kill a man who was once a brother. Kill the link between you and them. Kill him as your enemy, as our enemy. Prove your loyalty to us," Corsi says, every word spit out like venom.

This is the moment I decide who I am. I decide what is worth it and what isn't.

Hayes can't help me. Gage can't save me. I'm on my own. This is my decision. And I won't let them ever take any blame for this decision. It is mine and mine alone.

I already know what I'm going to do. I knew what my decision would be the second I realized what was going to be asked of me.

It feels like years have passed since Corsi told me what my blood oath would be, but it's only been a second or two.

I never relish killing. As stone-faced and emotionless as I am when I do kill others, it affects me every time. I know my exact count. I know every person I've ever killed, I know what it does to me, and I know how it affects the world of the person I killed.

I've made my decision. And everyone in this room knows what I'm going to do too.

Call me a heartless, cruel bastard. I know I'm damned to hell. No amount of forgiveness will absolve me of what I'm about to do or what I've done in the past.

I also know that if I do this, the Retribution Kings will become my enemy. They will demand retribution. They will hunt me down to the end of my days. The only escape will be to destroy all of them.

And yet, it doesn't change my mind.

I grab my gun.

Lift it.

Aim.

And fire.

A high-pitched gasp sounds behind me.

I don't have to turn around to know whose voice that is. Still, I don't react. I'm as emotionless as ever.

But inside, my heart drops at her shock.

I turn slowly, watching Rialta stare at me. I see the surprise, the fear, the anguish on her face. This is an image of me that will stay with her forever.

That's what breaks me. My job to make her fall in love with me or show my love for her just got harder. If she didn't already hate me, she will now. She'll think of me as a monster—a ruthless beast incapable of love.

And she'd be right.

CHAPTER 14

Rialta

"I **KNOW** you don't understand why I arranged this marriage, why you can't choose your own husband, or why you had to give your boyfriend up." Vincent pauses. "I know you don't even truly believe that I love you." He takes a deep breath as if it pains him. Suddenly, I see how much older he looks than the last time I saw him. His hair is whiter, his face paler and gaunter.

He pulls me into a hug, and I hug him back. He's the father I always wanted, and the father I always hated. He is everything I've ever wanted to have and everything I wanted to stay away from.

Every day that I was gone, I wanted my family back, my real family. Him and River are it. They are my real family. And I know everything he's done has been to protect me—even in his own fucked up way.

"I hope someday you understand why I'm forcing you into this marriage. And you'll realize it was the right decision." He pulls back and looks at me with tears in his eyes. I've never seen him so vulnerable looking. "And if you never come to understand my decision or agree with it, then I hope you can someday forgive me."

I don't know what to say to that. I can't forgive him for what he's making me do. And I definitely don't understand how this benefits me.

I give him a soft smile, and then he says, "It's time."

I suck in a breath, knowing this time will be different. Last time, during my attempted marriage to Beckett, I almost died from poisoning. This time, death won't save me.

I won't die.

There won't be an attempt on my life.

I won't be saved in any way. Vincent, River, and Beckett have made sure of it. I will be protected. I will be safe. And once married, I know that Lennox will protect me.

Safe.

I should feel good knowing I might live much longer than I ever expected. My marriage will ensure my safety. I will have someone with me who has vowed to do whatever it takes to keep me safe, but it doesn't make me feel any better. I don't enjoy the feeling of being safe.

I want freedom. I want risk. I want excitement. I want my own life.

I pick up my bouquet, and then I take my father's arm, and he leads me out of the small dressing room toward the back of the church, where I see River is standing, waiting to proceed. She's wearing a simple red dress that hugs her curves and shows off the slightest baby bump. She looks radiant and beautiful, but I know beneath the waves of fabric are guns, knives, and all sorts of weapons she will use without hesitation on anyone that threatens me or her baby.

I smile at her, reassuring her I'm okay, and she doesn't need to worry about me.

She looks at me a second longer, concern written on her face, but then Vincent's men open the back doors, and she starts walking down the aisle. We give her a moment to walk, and then Vincent leads me to the doors, where we start walking down the long aisle together.

I thought every step would feel like immense dread—like I was walking to my own funeral instead of my wedding. I thought it would take immense effort to take each step toward Lennox.

Instead, it's easy—far too easy.

I don't look at Lennox or the others at the end of the aisle at first. My thoughts are back in the basement where I saw Lennox fulfill the blood oath.

I heard the voices from downstairs when I was getting ready with River. She tried to stop me from going down there, but I had to know. I had to see what Lennox vowed.

I both saw enough and didn't see enough. I don't know the exact vows or the deal he struck with my father, but I saw the determination, the power, and the heavy heart Lennox used to take a life.

He didn't take it easily. He showed the respect a life is owed, but he also wasn't afraid to do what needed to be done. He did the task and took the pain, the guilt, and the burden on himself. I know he will carry that death with him as he does every other death caused by his own hand.

When Lennox spotted me, I saw his heart being crushed. It was only a flicker, but it was enough that I saw. He isn't heartless or cruel like my father is when he kills. He hated that I saw that part of him. It's the part he does because it's the job, but he takes no real pleasure in it.

I gasped at the sight of watching a man die. It isn't the first time I've seen someone die, and it won't be the last, but it's still shocking every time it happens. It makes me think I'm not cut out for this world.

Suddenly, we are at the end of the aisle.

I haven't looked up. I haven't really registered the others

until this moment. I noticed River standing as my maid of honor with far too happy of an expression on her face. She is blissfully happy about becoming a mom, and she thinks my marrying Lennox is for the best. But I'm going to give her hell later for looking so happy on a day that feels somber to me.

And then I look at the three guys standing behind Lennox. Hayes, then Gage, then Beckett—all of them looking sharp in their black tuxes. Hayes gives me a wink, while the others look on more solemnly. I appreciate the seriousness, but it's Hayes' wink that almost gets me to smile. *Damn him.*

And then I look at Lennox. He's wearing the same tux as the others, but somehow standing here like this, he seems to tower over the others in both size and attractiveness. The tux fits him perfectly, and his muscles bulge around the biceps. His hair is swept to one side, and his tattoos creep up his neck and arms in a sexy tease. His expression is mostly unreadable, like he's waiting in line at a bank—slightly bored and unfeeling. But on closer inspection, I see more. I see the ways his pupils flick over mine, searching to see how I feel. I see his breath leave his body as he truly takes in my body up close.

Everyone assumed I'd want a princess ballgown dress. Maybe the old me would have chosen such a dress, but the new me—the one who is determined to take fate into her own hands and not be a damsel in distress—wanted something sexy and grown up. I chose a mermaid-style dress with a high neckline in front and low-cut in the back. It's a simple dress with very few embellishments, but it hugs all of my curves and makes me feel elegant and sexy, which is what I wanted.

Now with Lennox's all-intensive gaze on me, I'm pretty sure I should have worn a potato sack.

I blush, hoping the others don't notice my reaction to his gaze. The little lift in Lennox's lip tells me he notices, and he still thinks he's going to win that stupid bet of ours.

He can be as hot and flirtatious, and gorgeous as he wants. He could shower me with compliments. He could bribe me with gifts. It won't matter. I'm in love with Kit. And even if I wasn't in love with Kit, I could still figure out a way to ignore Lennox's advances.

He gives me the slightest shake of the head combined with a soft smirk that says he's going to enjoy our challenge. But then his mischievous eyes grow serious again as he holds out his hand to me.

This is the moment when I accept my fate. This is the moment where I decide to become his wife or run. This is my last chance to back out.

And looking at Lennox and the others, I'm pretty sure if I decided to run, they'd do everything within their power to help me. But it wouldn't be enough. This would still eventually be the outcome. My father won't let it be any other way. He's far too afraid of me living on my own. He's afraid I'll die. And the most important thing to him is that I stay alive, and the Corsi name continues on.

I want to stay alive—so I'll trust his decision in Lennox keeping me alive. But I won't continue the Corsi line. *It ends with me.*

I take Lennox's hand without hesitation. And I can feel everyone smiling at my decision, everyone except Lennox.

Lennox looks terrified. Apparently, he didn't think this would really happen until now.

He cocks his head to his side, and I realize maybe he's reacting to my own expression, but I feel nothing but content with my decision. This feels like my decision.

'You okay?' Lennox mouths as he takes my other hand after I hand my bouquet to River.

I narrow my eyes, not sure why he's asking me that question. Then I see his pained stare. He's not concerned that I might be upset about marrying him. He's concerned about what I witnessed in the basement.

I nod.

He opens his mouth, wanting to say more, but then the ceremony starts, and he bites his lip, changing his mind.

I don't know what he thinks. Maybe he thought I would change my mind and not marry him after seeing him kill someone. I always knew he's killed people before, and I know he will in the future. But seeing him actually do it, it did change how I view him—just not for the worst.

Maybe that says something about me. I'm just as much of a monster at heart as he is. I have too much of Vincent's blood in my veins. Maybe Lennox and I are more alike than I first realized.

The rest of the wedding goes by in a blur.

Our vows.

Exchanging rings.

And then it's over except for one thing.

"You may now kiss the bride," the officiant says.

I hold my breath as my heart stops. This is the moment I've been dreading, where I've truly betrayed Kit and my own heart. It's one thing to be married to a man on paper, but another to be physically intimate with him.

Lennox starts to lean in, and I go rigid. Maybe if I don't participate I won't feel like I'm a cheater and I've lost control of everything.

I close my eyes, readying my lips for the invasion, when I feel his lips land on the palm of my hand.

My eyes flicker open, and I stare at a smirking Lennox. His eyes tell me the dirty things he really wants to do to me in private when I finally give in to him.

I smile—genuinely for the first time in what feels like forever.

I can feel my father's eyes staring at us in disapproval, along with the rest of the Corsi family. Lennox took a huge risk in not kissing me like he was supposed to. It's the smallest act of defiance, the smallest act of making this wedding our own.

And it could lead to the Corsi men seeing it as a flagrant disregard for tradition. That he's marrying me but won't really be married to me.

I want to hug Lennox and thank him for trying to protect me, but I know he can't not touch me in public forever. He's only brought me a temporary reprieve, but at least it means that when we are physical it will be on our terms and not in front of hundreds of people because it's what's expected of us.

The officiant doesn't seem phased; he just continues on. "And now I'd like to introduce you to Mr. and Mrs. Lennox Corsi."

Lennox tightens his grip on my hand, and for once, I feel like we are in this together. Then we run down the aisle together like two school-aged kids playing together in the park.

CHAPTER 15

Lennox

IT WAS NEVER my intention not to kiss her. I expected to do everything by the book, do nothing to make these people not like me. I know I have to tread carefully if I don't want to end up dead.

But with one look at Rialta, I wanted to give her this one thing. I didn't want to kiss her for the first time in front of everyone. I didn't want to take that from her. If I had my choice, she'd choose when she would kiss me for the first time.

We don't have a lot of time. I will be expected to kiss her, among other things. Maybe we should have planned ahead and kissed before the wedding so it wouldn't have felt so big in front of everyone. Maybe I should have just done a quick brush of our lips together and not made a big deal out of it.

If I want to make Rialta fall in love with me, then giving her this gift was the best way to help that, especially after she saw the monster I had to be in the basement.

Still, the look on Corsi's face told me he wasn't pleased with my decision. And there were plenty of snickers in the crowd as we ran hand in hand down the aisle that told me I will never be respected as the new mob boss.

I'll worry about that later, but I knew I wouldn't have a chance at Rialta's heart if I took this from her. She was terrified of that kiss, so I know I made the right decision.

I lead Rialta into a room at the back of the church as the others start coming down the aisle. The room gives us a moment of privacy before the reception, a moment to decide on how we are going to tackle it together.

"Thank you," she says, biting her bottom lip.

"Don't thank me. I forced you to marry me. And I made a bet with you that I wouldn't rape you—I'd seduce you."

"A kiss is far from rape, but still, thank you."

I put my hands in my pocket, watching her as she twirls the two rings now on her finger—one opal jewel and one rose gold band.

I stare down at my own silver ring that feels cold and foreign on my hand.

"I can't not kiss you forever, though. I wish I could let you decide *when* you kiss me."

"*If*," she says, smirking.

"When or *if* you kiss me. But I can't, not without risking everything."

She nods, as if she already knew this, but doesn't say more on the topic. "What vows did you make to my father? To his men?"

I shake my head. "It doesn't matter."

She sighs. "I thought for a moment we were going to be a team now. That not kissing me meant we were going to make decisions together, but I see that's not true."

I rub the back of my neck. "I want that, but there are some things that are better if you don't know."

She stares at me long and hard, as if trying to decide if my words are true. Then she walks over to me, taking her sweet time, swaying her hips as she walks and drawing my eyes to every glorious curve on her body.

She's absolutely stunning. I've always known she is beautiful, but before today, I always thought of her as a childish girl, not an attractive woman. There is no denying what she is today, though. In another other circumstance, I would be hitting on her with the intention of taking her to my bed tonight.

She'll be in my bed, but too bad sleep will be all that's going to happen. No matter how much charm I lay on her tonight, she won't touch me or let me touch her once the bedroom doors close.

"We should set some boundaries and expectations for the reception—" I start, but stop rambling as she continues walking toward me.

My mouth falls open as I stare at her glide across the floor to me. It was magical watching her walk down the aisle. Her gaze didn't meet mine until the last second, which meant I had ample time to look at her without her realizing just how drawn I am to her.

But right now, with her eyes locked on mine, there is no hiding my feelings. I'm usually the best at keeping my emotions under control, but right now, they're screaming all over my face.

She stops suddenly, looking up at me with her big brown eyes as if waiting for something.

"You're so beautiful, Rialta. Sometimes I wish we had met differently, and maybe then I'd have a real chance with you. Maybe then we wouldn't drive each other crazy. I would have said you are the most gorgeous woman I'd ever seen, and I had to have you," I say sadly because it's true.

I'm not trying to flatter her; I'm just being honest. But the circumstances are what they are, and neither of us will ever give the other a real chance. My heart is locked away in steel, and hers belongs to another man.

Rialta grabs the back of my neck and looks me dead in the eye. "This isn't me losing our bet—this is me taking control and not giving those bastards anything."

Her lips crash down on mine. For a kiss that isn't really meant to be a kiss, Rialta kisses me hard. Any kiss after this will feel benign and gentle in comparison. This kiss is meant to punish us as much as it is about taking control. *Damn, do I find that sexy.*

I grab her neck back, holding her tightly to my lips so she can feel all of me. She'll never be surprised again when it comes to kissing me.

Our tongues meld and mix together in a bitter battle. Quickly I feel the reaction I want from her—sweet surrender.

With this kiss, she's accepted her fate, accepted our marriage.

I don't know if she's ready to give Kit up yet.

I don't know if she's ready to take on any of the responsibilities that are expected of her as my wife and mafia queen.

But this is definitely a start.

She pulls away, leaving us both gasping and wanting more.

"You're attracted to me? I always thought you hated me," she says quietly, feeling the energy of our kiss.

"I'm attracted to you. And I hate you."

She laughs at that. "Ditto."

I raise my eyebrows.

"Calm down. I'm attracted to Ryan Gosling, too; it doesn't mean I'm going to cheat on my boyfriend with him."

I invade her space, enjoying watching her sharp inhale as I do. I love how much I affect her.

"Yes, but it means I have a chance. If you thought I was a hideous monster, then there would be no hope of winning our bet."

"Why do you want to win so badly?"

I take a step back and put my hands in my pocket, staring at her. "Isn't it obvious?"

"No." Her eyes search mine for the answer.

"I want to fuck you. I want to see you pregnant with my babies. I'm a fucking caveman, and I want you."

"Oh," her lips part, and her cheeks pink.

"And I think deep down, you want an excuse to fuck me too."

She frowns. "In your dreams."

I shrug. "And nightmares," I mutter under my breath. "So what are we going to do about this reception?"

She sighs and goes back to fidgeting with her rings. Suddenly, she looks at me with new determination in her eyes. "Play the part."

———

Play the part.

I've never been very good at acting. I'm always just stone-faced and emotionless. But when Rialta suggests we become the people expected of us tonight, I can't resist going along with it. For one, it will probably save my ass from being beaten for not kissing her. And two, I'll take any excuse to have my hands all over her.

A few minutes later, we're strutting into the reception room at The Langham hotel, hand in hand, once again being announced as Mr. and Mrs. Lennox Corsi. It's weird; in one day, I've given up everything—my family, my name, my singledom.

I can already see the smirks of the men in the room who

think Rialta has me by the balls after I didn't kiss her in front of everyone.

That changes now.

I grab Rialta's ass and yank her toward me roughly. She squeals out of breath before I slam my lips down on hers, my tongue invading her mouth as I do.

The crowd is silent for a second, unsure how to react. But when I end the kiss with a wicked desire of what I'm going to do with her soon in my eyes, they all whoop and holler. In return, Rialta's eyes light up with her own yearning and a touch of defiant fire.

I continue to hold onto her ass as we are led to the head table, where two chairs are placed for us to have dinner. I sit down in my chair first, not being gentlemanly at all.

As Rialta is about to take her own seat, I motion for her to sit on my lap instead. Grabbing her hips, I guide her down to my lap, as she gives me an 'I'm going to make you pay for that later' glare.

I shrug, knowing I'm going to enjoy whatever punishment she tries to inflict later. I'm enjoying this little game of ours too much already.

Our friends are seated at a table to our right, and I do my best not to look in their direction. Hayes is likely cracking up at the sight of us, while the others are probably looking on with too much amusement. They know it's all just an act, but we aren't doing it for them.

We are playing along so the rest of the men in this room will think of me as they do Vincent Corsi—a strong, merciless leader who will do whatever it takes to bring in money and continue their decades of customs and traditions.

Two glasses of Dom are placed in front of us. We each sip our glass as I wrap one arm around her neck possessively. My hand rests just above her collarbone, and I stroke her neck over and over again, enjoying seeing little tiny shivers and goosebumps on her arms.

I lean into her neck and lick from her shoulder to her earlobe, biting down sharply on her ear when I reach it.

She yelps and whispers discreetly behind her glass of champagne, "Play nice."

"Why? I know you like it. I can see every reaction your body makes to my touch. And if I had to bet, you're drenched for me between those legs."

She scoots her ass over my crotch, rubbing a little too roughly, and eliciting a moan.

She smirks. "And somebody already has his erection on full display."

"I've never denied that I find you hot. I want to fuck you, and I will."

"That's just all you want from me—a woman who will be at your beck and call to fuck you whenever you want and nothing more. Don't pretend you aren't just like every asshole in this room. Just because you didn't kiss me at the ceremony doesn't mean you aren't a bastard."

I don't say anything because she's right. If we were to ever have sex, that's all I'd want from her—not a real relationship.

Vincent spends the evening giving speech after speech, toast after toast, as food and alcohol pour in. There's dancing and mingling and more groping and teasing between Rialta and me until finally, she's exhausted from the charade and being on her feet.

She yawns while I dance with her, smashing our bodies together.

"I think it's time I get you to bed," I say.

She shakes her head. "I don't want to go to bed." She yawns again.

"If I don't get you to bed, you're going to fall asleep in my arms on the dance floor."

I start to drag her off the floor.

"Wait," she says with panic in her eyes.

I frown and look from her to where she's staring. In the corner is Vincent Corsi and one of his top men, Andrea.

They nod at us solemnly.

Rialta freezes in her tracks.

And now I'm holding onto her not to put on an act but to keep her from falling to the ground.

"What's wrong?" I whisper into her hair.

She doesn't respond.

Andrea walks over to us. "If you'll follow me, I'll show you to your room."

"I think that would be a good idea," I say and hold Rialta around the waist, moving her forward. I still don't understand what's wrong with her as we follow him.

As we pass them, I spot River grasping Beckett's hand like a vise grip to keep herself from running to Rialta. I try to read the motive for her concern, but I assume it's just because she knows Rialta so well and can see her distress. Hayes and Gage watch us pass with trepidation.

Am I missing something?

Andrea leads us out of the ballroom and ushers us through a nearby door.

I frown, confused why we aren't being led to a honeymoon or penthouse suite. I would have expected Vincent Corsi to have gone all out for tonight.

As I help Rialta inside the nearly empty room, Andrea looks at me with vicious eyes and at Rialta with far too much delight as she cowers in fear.

"We'll be waiting for the proof," Andrea says with a devilish wink before closing the door. I realize far too late what's expected of us tonight. We may have had our own bet and rules, but it doesn't matter. The Corsi mafia has their own rules—rules we will be expected to abide by or face severe consequences.

I don't know if I'll be able to protect her this time. And if I can't protect her, there is no way she will ever love me. Either way this turns out, my death is inevitable.

CHAPTER 16

Rialta

THE ROOM CONSISTS of a king bed and nothing else. No bathroom. No closet. No end table or lamps. No wall decorations. Just white walls and white bedding.

I knew this ritual would come. Secret and yet not very secret—it is expected, and yet the details are vague, even now. I don't know exactly what *proof* is required. I don't know if there are cameras, and we are being watched, or if they are just listening through doors and walls. I don't know if blood on the sheets is what is expected—proof of my virginity that was long ago taken.

I don't know. But something is expected, something dark and sinister. They want proof that Lennox is capable of being the true monster he is and will use his power over me, just like he was forced to do in that basement.

How can I save myself? It's far too late to stop this. We can't scheme like we did before. We have very few options left.

I don't blame Lennox for what he's going to do. He naively tried to make a bet with me, thinking he could seduce me into wanting him before he fucked me. He isn't a rapist by heart, but when push comes to shove, he'll become one. I have no doubt. Everything he's ever wanted is on the line.

I try to hide my fear, but I'm not good at keeping my emotions at bay like Lennox. I force myself to look at him, to prepare for what's about to happen. I shiver as I witness confusion quickly give way to the same evil wickedness I saw in the basement slithering over all of his features. His face starts to turn red, his eyes fade into black, and a low growl bounces through the small room.

I close my eyes, pretending I can block everything out. I won't feel anything. I won't end up destroyed through this process. I won't hurt Kit. Everything I am won't become lost in a single night.

Lennox whooshes past me, not touching me.

I peek one eye open just a little bit and see Lennox jump up in the corner of the room, his hand sweeping until he finds the tiny camera pointed toward the bed. He tosses it on the floor and stomps his foot on it, shattering it.

My heart starts to slow, and my breath becomes more even. *Maybe he'll find a way to protect me after all.*

I'll owe him. Not sex or heirs, but I'll owe him some kind of protection if he finds a way to save me tonight.

He sweeps every corner of the room, finding one more camera he breaks under his foot. His eyes scan the room furiously, trying to find any other hidden cameras.

When he seems satisfied, he pulls his phone out and starts texting someone. Gage, I hope. If there are any cameras left in the room, Gage would be able to find them and disable them even remotely.

The cameras are taken care of, but it won't be enough to save me. They'll be able to hear through the walls and doors. And they'll still want proof.

My heart starts racing again, but at least now we can

whisper in privacy and make a plan. We can come up with some sort of proof to save us both.

I open my mouth to speak, but Lennox doesn't wait for my words.

He pounces.

He grabs me roughly and shoves me down hard on the bed.

"I'm going to enjoy this. I'm going to enjoy finding out if you're a virgin or not, Rialta. You better hope you are because, one way or another, I'm going to enjoy watching you bleed." He's become a different man in the blink of an eye.

"Lennox," I whisper softly, trying to remind him who he is, trying to break through the rage that has taken hold of him. It's one thing to fuck me against my will, but I expected him to be gentle and flirtatious and as kind as he could be when he took me.

This—I didn't expect this.

His nostrils flare wide, and he's breathing heavily as he removes his jacket and tie, standing to the side of the bed, his eyes never leaving mine.

I squirm up the bed, tucking my knees against my chest, trying to get as far away from him as possible.

"Lennox," I try again, but my voice is too quiet. "I'll fuck you; just give me time to warm up."

"You don't need time. I know how wet you are. I know how turned on you were the entire evening. You want this, but I want to hear you beg first."

I blink, trying to rack my brain for how to stop this. *How do I break through to him? Did I just entirely misjudge him? How could I have been so wrong?*

He kicks his shoes off next, then undoes the buttons down his shirt, one by one. He's milking every moment, like he's just undressing, not about to hurt me.

I swallow hard, my brain going a million miles an hour trying to come up with some sort of plan. *How do I get free?* But I'm blanking. I can't think. I don't understand what's happening. *How could I be so foolish?*

Run.

It's the only thing that comes to mind.

I wait until he starts walking toward the bed. He's shirtless but still wearing pants, and then I run for the door.

Run, run, run.

I make it to the door.

I grab the handle.

But he slams his body into me, my front pressed against the door as his hardness hits me from behind.

"Please," I beg.

"Please, what? Please, fuck you?" Lennox growls.

I beat my fists against the door. "Help! Someone, please!"

"I like it when you beg," he cackles.

Then I hear the rip of my dress from behind, and I know I'm completely exposed. He could be inside of me within seconds.

Instead, I feel him crash his body against me again. I can feel his hardness in his pants against the back of my panties.

His hand twists into my hair, gabbing it as he moans against my neck.

"Please," I whisper.

His hand slaps against my ass hard enough that tears sting my cheeks. I can't keep them in as I sob against the door.

And then my panties are on the floor as his hand slaps my bare ass. I can't help but yelp.

I'm limp as he drags me back to the bed by my hair. His body quickly covers mine as the bed creaks loudly under our combined weight.

He growls like I've never heard a man growl. Low and deep, shaking all the walls.

I tremble beneath him, scared of just how much he's going to tear me apart.

I hear a rip.

Then I watch as Lennox takes out a knife.

My eyes widen, and I go deadly still.

He slices into his own chest, just above his heart—where a Retribution King tattoo sits. Blood spills out as if he's denouncing his family and claiming a new one.

He tears a sheet in his hands, and the next thing I know, he's reached between my legs, smearing the sheet between them and coating them with my wetness.

I hiss as he does, a last act of defiance. He's so cruel to take any natural lubricant that could possibly make this enjoyable for me.

But then his hand is gone. I see him use the same sheet to clean up the blood from his chest.

He's off the bed.

Putting his shirt and jacket back on.

Slipping into his shoes.

Tie around his neck.

Sheet in hand—bloodied, sweaty, and stained with my wetness.

And then Lennox walks out of the room without a word to me.

"Here's your proof," I hear him growl. "Now leave me and my *wife* the fuck alone."

I hear grumbling slowly die down from outside.

Lennox doesn't reenter the bedroom.

I'm still lying on the bed. My ass stings. My dress is torn. The sheets I'm lying on are shredded. I'm flushed and sweating. Tears and mascara are dripping down my face.

I see one of Vincent's men poke their heads inside for

the briefest of moments, and I grab for the remaining covers, trying to fully cover myself.

He just nods at me and closes the door, leaving me all alone.

I curl up in a ball—waiting for what comes next. But no one comes for me.

Not Lennox.

Not River.

Not any of the guys.

Not Vincent.

Not his men.

I'm alone and violated and broken.

It takes me longer than I want to admit to realize that I'm not broken at all. I'm completely intact. I'm safe. All Lennox did was scare me to show me what he is capable of.

But he protected me—in his own way. The only way he could come up with. He protected me without ruining his chance of becoming Vincent's successor. *He protected me,* I repeat over and over again as I drift off to sleep. And now I owe my husband my protection.

CHAPTER 17

Lennox

I **KNOCK** on the door at six in the morning. She's probably still asleep, but I want to get out of here as soon as possible.

"Come in," I hear Rialta's voice quietly through the door. I don't know how she knows it's me or someone she trusts. I'm guessing the fact that I knocked at all instead of barging in gave her some clue.

She's lying on the bed, curled up in a ball, still in her torn wedding dress with the thin sheet pulled up around her.

I drop her bag on the floor. "Get changed, and then we can go. Ri wants to invite us over to celebrate."

She nods, looking at me with a tight expression. Her eyes search mine for any warmth, any kindness—she'll find none. I left all my kindness in this room last night. I'm not a nice person. In time, she'll see that if she hasn't realized it already.

I walk back out of the room, giving her some privacy to get dressed. It takes her a while, but eventually, she opens the door.

I scan her jeans, thin cream sweater, and messy bun. Her

makeup is gone, along with the mascara that stained her cheeks. There is no evidence left of what transpired here last night.

"Ready?" I ask, a little too snappy.

"Yes," she breathes impatiently.

As we drive to Ri and Beckett's apartment, Rialta breathes steadily, staring out the window for most of the trip. She's probably thinking about everything that happened last night, while I try to block it all out and forget it ever happened.

"Thank y—"

"Don't," I snap.

"What?"

"Don't thank me, *ever*." I bring the car to a halt in Ri and Beckett's building garage.

She frowns and reaches over to touch my arm, but I've already unbuckled my seatbelt and climbed out.

She does the same, and we head into Ri and Beckett's condo in silence. We find them in their living room, along with Gage and Hayes. There are mimosas, bloody marys, brunch food, and celebratory decorations.

Everyone stares at us as we enter. We're no longer touching since we no longer have to put on a show. Although, none of them knows what really happened last night. No one knows if we had consensual sex, if I raped her, or if it was all fake, and I never touched her in that way. No one knows what kind of monster I am. No one knows the pleasure I got from seeing her in pain and the fear in her voice. I crave that darkness. Not fucking her against her will took everything inside of me to stop and not hurt her.

I look from one face to the next, waiting for someone to hate me the way they should, for someone to try and kick my ass for hurting Rialta. Instead, I get reassuring smiles from each and every one of them, especially Ri. She smiles at me as if she knows I did something to protect Rialta when I did no such thing. I hurt her even if I could have hurt her more.

I grab a bloody mary and walk out onto the balcony, needing my space. I can't be here celebrating. With Hayes and Gage celebrating that I'm one step closer to my plan. With Ri and Beckett thinking I'm what's best to protect Rialta. With Ri secretly hoping we'll fall in love. I don't deserve any of their praise.

Beckett walks outside a few minutes later.

"You okay?" he asks.

"No."

"Want to talk about it?"

"No."

He stands out on the balcony a few minutes longer, waiting to see if I want to talk. When I don't say anything, don't so much as even look at him, he goes back inside.

With the exception of getting more drinks, I stay outside until the sun begins to set, lost in my thoughts and memories.

When I go back inside, I see Rialta and Ri talking happily. Rialta puts her hand on Ri's growing bump, and the two laugh.

"Ready?" I ask in Rialta's direction.

Rialta looks at me and then nods. She says her goodbyes, while I sulk and walk out without saying goodbye to anyone. I'm not in the mood for small talk.

Back in my car, it's back to silence.

Same in the elevator as I carry her bag up to my apartment.

Nothing as we enter my apartment.

"You can have the bedroom for now. I'll sleep downstairs on the couch," I say, after I take her bag upstairs and set it in the closet. There should be plenty of space for her to unpack there.

I start to head back downstairs when she grabs my forearm.

I flinch at her touch and squeeze my eyes shut as the darkness creeps in.

Death.

Destruction.

Loss.

Dark hair being tangled, pulled, ripped.

Her bare skin bloodied and bruised.

Her cries higher and sharper.

My soul being ripped apart.

I shake off her touch and push the darkness out. When I open my eyes, she's staring at me with concern.

"Where'd you go just then?" she asks.

"Nowhere."

She frowns. "Talk to me. I'm your wife now. I know our relationship is complicated, to say the least, but you can always talk to me."

"No."

"We need to talk about what happened last night. We need—"

"No, we don't need to talk about last night. It's done and over. There is nothing we can do to change it. We both got what we wanted."

She raises an eyebrow. "I got what I wanted?"

I look at the stairs. All I want is to go downstairs and collapse on the couch. I didn't sleep a second last night. Now that Rialta is safe in my apartment, I just want to sleep.

"You got more than you could have hoped for," I whisper.

"Talk to me. Please."

Please—that word triggers me. *I see her being dragged away. I'm bloodied on the floor and can barely open my eyes.*

She's being taken away. I'll never see her again. The last word she says to me is 'please.'

Rialta wraps her arms around me, pulling me into a tight hug before I can refuse her.

"Let. Go. Of. Me."

"No, not until you talk to me. Not until you tell me about last night. Not until you tell me what happens when your eyes gloss over, and you go cold and still. Not until you let me thank you."

I shake her off. "You shouldn't thank me. Go to sleep and we'll talk tomorrow."

It's a lie. I don't ever want to talk to her—not now and not tomorrow.

"I'm not tired."

"Then read a book or something, but I need to sleep."

I turn to walk downstairs, done with this conversation, when she says something just to get under my skin.

"Fine, then I'll call Kit. I'm not tired, and you won't talk to me, but he will."

I snap my head in her direction and shoot daggers at her with my eyes.

She smirks, knowing exactly what she's doing, exactly how she's getting under my skin.

"Go to sleep," I say, not playing into her games.

"I'm not tired."

"Go. To. Sleep." I growl, getting in her face and unleashing the devil within. I don't touch her, but I don't have to in order to make her fear me.

"I'm not afraid of you."

"You should be."

"I'm not. And I shouldn't be."

"You should be. You have no idea what I'm capable of. What you saw last night—that was nothing. That was a

Tuesday for me. The things you've seen Vincent do—I'm worse."

She looks at me with a soft gaze. "You're not."

"I am. You saw me kill an innocent man."

"He wasn't innocent," she counters.

"He didn't deserve to die."

"No one does, but we all die eventually," she shrugs casually.

I shake my head, letting the viciousness spread through me as I back her into a corner. My body pushes her without making physical contact.

"Last night, I wasn't in control."

"You were—"

"No, I wasn't in control. I unleashed who I was in order to have the kind of anger I needed to be believable."

I slam my hands on the wall behind her head, making her jump. "I hurt you. And I was seconds away from hurting you worse, maiming you so badly that you would never recover. You would have finally understood the true meaning of hating me. You're not safe with me. I'm not your protector, so don't thank me. Next time, I won't be able to hold onto the little bit of control I have."

I release my hands slowly and walk toward the stairs.

"No, you weren't."

I pause and look back at her.

"You weren't about to rape me. And you didn't hurt me."

She's wrong, so wrong, but I don't correct her. I just go downstairs and hope that, for once she does as she's told and goes to sleep.

CHAPTER 18

Rialta

I COME DOWNSTAIRS in one of Lennox's clean white T-shirts and black boxer briefs. I was too lazy to dig out my own pajamas last night. And I'm too exhausted from tossing and turning all night to bother putting on clothes or even untangling my hair. I tuck my phone into the waistband of the briefs before heading downstairs.

I barely slept last night. All I could think about was his pain and heartache. I don't understand what he lost, but he feels it all the way to his bones. And he feels responsible for the loss. He failed whoever was taken from him before—that much is clear.

I temporarily went insane last night, feeling like he actually cared about me. I actually felt like a fool for not breaking things off with Kit and trying to make a go with Lennox. He was kind when he didn't need to be, and we are stuck in this marriage for the long haul. It would be best for everyone if Lennox and I were to get along.

But after his reaction last night, I know why I'll cling to Kit with every part of my being. Lennox got under my skin last night, but I won't let it happen again.

I take a deep breath near the bottom of the stairs, prepared to deal with a grumpy Lennox. I loudly hop down the last step, hoping the sound will awaken Lennox.

"He's not here," a male voice says from the kitchen.

I stare at the couch to find it in perfect condition. Apparently, Lennox didn't sleep there last night. Turning toward the kitchen, I find Hayes has breakfast prepared on a plate and is pouring a cup of coffee.

"Oh," I say, walking toward one of the two kitchen bar stools.

"He's one of those people who wakes up before noon," Hayes says with a mischievous grin.

"It's much earlier than noon," I say, glancing around, trying to find a clock.

"Barely," Hayes grins. "I should have made you lunch instead of breakfast."

I eye the breakfast sandwich and smell the coffee. "Breakfast food is my favorite. I'd eat it for lunch and dinner, too, if I could."

"Then, good thing I made breakfast. How do you take your coffee?"

"Just black is fine."

He nods and places the plate and coffee in front of me. Then he pours himself a cup of coffee and sits next to me.

"Thank you." I take a bite. "Mmm, this is delicious."

"I know."

I laugh. "You aren't cocky or arrogant at all."

He shrugs. "I'm a good chef. No one has ever turned down my cooking."

"Ever wanted to be a chef full-time?"

"Why would I want to do that? I get to work my own hours, get paid well, and hang out with my best friends?"

I take another bite and speak with my mouth full. "I don't know, maybe the little part about being able to go home every night and know you won't die or have to kill anyone."

"Well, that sounds boring," he grins at me.

I smile back at Hayes. His smile is infectious, and he's incredibly likable.

I take another bite and moan. "Why couldn't I have married you instead of Lennox? I'd be happy to marry you if it meant I could eat your delicious cooking all the time."

"That can be arranged," Lennox says from behind me, making me jump.

I bite my lip nervously and turn to face him, while Hayes just continues looking from me to Lennox with his amused, happy grin on his face.

"Great! What do you say, sweetheart? Want to divorce this scoundrel and marry me instead?" Hayes teases, leaning in and kissing me unexpectedly on the lips.

My eyes never leave Lennox. He's good at hiding his feelings, but I swear I saw his jaw twitch when Hayes's lips touched mine. A second later, his face is wiped clean and expressionless. Maybe I imagined it or hoped that I can get under his skin as easily as he can mine.

"Where have you been this morning?" I ask Lennox.

"Dealing with business."

"What business?"

"None of your concern."

He's not going to talk to me anymore today than he did last night. He's still silent on all the things that matter.

I turn to Hayes. "What are you doing this morning?"

"Planning our wedding," Hayes winks.

I give him a weak grin. "How about teaching me some self-defense instead?"

Hayes glances at Lennox behind me and then nods after I assume Lennox gives him permission.

I sigh. I hate that this is my life now—getting permission from someone else to do the most basic of things.

Hayes stands up. "We have an apartment on this floor that we turned into a gym. We can go there. Get changed, and then I'll take you."

I look down at my clothes, knowing I don't have any workout clothes with me. Vincent didn't see the point of me having any other clothes. "Nah, I'm good."

Hayes looks to Lennox and then sighs.

"Okay, well, I guess that will have to do for now. Later we'll get you some proper workout clothes," Hayes says.

"Thank you." As I start to follow Hayes out of the apartment, I feel Lennox's eyes peering through my shirt. When he stares, I might as well not be wearing anything. I feel naked, like he can read through me.

He doesn't say anything but follows us to the door two down that Hayes unlocks.

We all step inside, and this room is different than the other two apartments. It has padding on the entire floor, with a large space in the center for what I assume is fighting practice. Various weights and gym equipment line the edges. This room also has no windows. Instead, a mirror is fixed on the wall where windows once were.

I stare at myself. I look like I just rolled out of Lennox's bed, and I guess, technically, I did. I look scrawny and puny beneath Lennox's oversized shirt. I don't look like I'm about to work out.

And still, this feels like the first right decision I've made in a long while. I pull out my phone and send Kit a quick text. Then I stretch my arms over my head, trying to prepare for what Hayes will teach me.

I hear the door open a second later and see Gage entering, whispering something to Lennox. They each have a mug of coffee in their hands as they pull up chairs on the edge of the mat. Apparently, they think whatever Hayes is going to try to teach me will be entertaining.

"So what do you know, gorgeous?" Hayes asks playfully.

I ignore his flirtatious shenanigans. "Nothing."

His smile drops. "It can't be nothing. You've grown up as Vincent Corsi's daughter. You were hunted your entire life. Ri was your best friend. They had to have taught you something."

"Vincent taught me nothing. That's why he employed Ri—she's the strong one, and I'm the weak one. Ri tried to teach me, but I was young, and it just didn't come naturally. She ran out of time before I was sent away."

Hayes looks from me to the guys behind me, raising his brows in disbelief.

"Okay, then." He pulls his hair up into a bun and adjusts his glasses. "I would love to start with the basics—form, strength, stamina—but given that someone is trying to kill you every other day, let's start with basic self-defense moves first, and you can simultaneously work on your overall strength."

"Okay."

"I'll show you some basic strikes first and then how to get out of a hold and bindings."

My cheeks heat slightly at the last time I was in bindings and how turned on I felt as Lennox tried to scare me.

"Rialta?" Hayes asks, waving his hand in front of my eyes.

"Yes?"

"Where did you go?" He grins so fucking wide. *How can someone smile so much and be this happy while knowing he could die any time he leaves his apartment?*

"Nowhere. I'm focused."

"Good."

Hayes moves my arms, legs, and core to help me into

different attack positions. He helps me keep my abs tight as I attack. He stands close and makes me laugh, and keeps me at ease as I try to strike him and fail miserably. I usually don't make contact with him, but if I do, I don't hit him hard enough to kill a fly on his body, let alone stop his attack.

Hayes doesn't say anything negative, though. He's nothing but encouraging and positive. He's a great motivational speaker. He could convince me I'm capable of flying an airplane after only an hour of practice—which isn't exactly a good thing.

I fall to the floor, somehow tripping instead of landing a swift kick to Hayes's groin like he showed me. I'm covered in sweat, my hair has fallen from my ponytail, and I'm exhausted.

Hayes extends his hand to me. "Not bad; let's give it another try."

"Not bad? That's the worst attempt at a kick I've ever seen. She's not going to fend off an attacker for even a second," Lennox says.

I gruff as I stand up. "If you think I'm so bad, then why don't you teach me?"

Lennox laughs. "I have no patience, unlike Hayes. I'm not good at motivational speeches, either. You wouldn't like me teaching you."

I ball my hands into fists, feeling anger welling inside me.

Hayes stands between me and Lennox, regaining my attention. "Let's try something different. Tell me what you're good at. Did you play any sports in high school? Were you a runner, a swimmer, a—"

"She's an artist. An excellent illustrator, painter, and sculptor," Kit says from the doorway.

I smile and run to him. It's been an exhausting couple of days. All I've wanted to do was see him, even though I'm technically married.

I throw my arms around his neck and pull him to me for a firm kiss. I'm safe. He's safe. *But how do I keep him safe?*

Give him up, the little voice in my head says.

I can't.

My heart constricts, holding him closer like a vice grip. I can't let him go. He's all I have left.

Kit's eyes are heavy and full of emotion as he holds me after I pull back from kissing him. He's been as worried as I have being apart, wondering if I'm still alive.

I hear a throat clear from behind me, but I don't move. This isn't about putting on a show or making Lennox mad; it's just what I need. It's what is necessary. I need to be close to Kit.

"Are we done with our lessons for today? If so, I at least want to give you a conditioning program to follow so you can build up some strength and endurance. You'll need it to throw a strong enough punch to protect yourself," Hayes says.

I'm about to say yes, I'm done with our lessons for today, but then I look at Kit.

"Actually, can you show Kit everything you just showed me?" I say, looking from Kit to Hayes.

Hayes just blinks, confounded.

"Show him how to defend himself. He was a wrestler in high school, so he already has some basics, and he's much stronger than I am. I can't defend him, but he can have the skills to defend himself and help protect me when you guys aren't around."

"We will always be around," Lennox growls, suddenly standing right beside me. He rests his hand on my shoulder, displaying his wedding ring even though he hasn't touched me since last night.

I grind my teeth together, as Kit stares at Lennox's hand with trepidation. "I agree that I won't purposely go out again without security, but there may come a time when it just happens. And it's better to be prepared for that inevitability. Kit should know some self-defense."

He probably also needs to know how to use a gun—we both do, but I'll approach that conversation another time.

"He doesn't. We will always be with you. I'm not letting you out of my sight again," Lennox growls, still gripping my shoulder.

"I know. But it will make me feel better if Kit knows some basic skills. You wouldn't want me jumping in front of a bullet to protect him, would you?" I step out of his grasp.

Lennox narrows his eyes at me. "Fine," he snaps, nodding at Hayes.

Lennox sits back in his chair, and I find a spot on the floor opposite them, while Hayes starts to teach Kit the basics.

Kit quickly catches on, blocking several attacks from Hayes and landing a few good punches of his own.

I grin, already feeling better about having Kit in my world. If he can protect himself, then I wouldn't feel as guilty. But it still has to be his decision, and I'm not sure what he'll choose. I'm not sure he'll choose me.

I bite my nails as I watch Kit throw a punch that knocks Hayes on his ass.

I clap and cheer, like I'm at a boxing match.

Gage claps.

Hayes grins, impressed.

Lennox stands up, wordlessly. He helps Hayes off the floor with a look of gloom over his face.

Lennox nods at Kit silently, an unspoken conversation happening between them.

Kit nods in return.

And then Kit attacks Lennox, throwing the same move that knocked Hayes on his ass.

Kit attacks again and again, but Lennox dodges and deflects as if I were the one throwing punches.

I hold my breath, unsure of what's about to happen. But I do know one thing—I was wrong in thinking Kit could defend himself. Watching Lennox fight him makes it painstakingly clear that Kit isn't ready for a real fight. *How foolish was I to think one lesson would prepare him?*

Kit's sweating and panting hard now, determined to knock Lennox on his ass. Meanwhile, Lennox could still be drinking his coffee in one hand while he pushes Kit around with the other. It no longer looks like an even match.

I'm not sure what to do, what to say.

Gage and Hayes look on with doom, like they know what's about to happen. Deep in my heart somewhere, I guess I know what's about to happen too.

Everything happens in slow motion—Kit's arm raising back, Lennox's lips lifting in a smirk, and then Lennox's fist ramming into Kit's nose.

Blood spews, and Kit falls hard to the ground—lifeless.

CHAPTER 19

Rialta

"KIT!" I scream as I run to his body on the floor. I'm sure he's fine, but seeing him fall limp to the floor does something to me. It strikes fear through my heart at the thought of this happening for real and it being all my fault.

I fall to my knees next to Kit as Lennox continues to tower over him, not caring in the least that he just hurt the man I love.

"Kit," I say again as I grab his shoulder and gently roll him over onto his back. As I cup Kit's head in my lap, Hayes kneels next to me.

"He's fine, just knocked out," Hayes says.

"What do I do?"

"He's breathing fine; just give him a minute. He'll have a nasty headache when he comes to and shouldn't be left alone for a while, but—"

Suddenly Kit's eyes flicker open.

I smile in relief. "You're okay."

Kit grins. "Of course, I'm okay." He reaches up and strokes my cheek, brushing away a tiny tear. "I'm looking at the most beautiful woman in the world."

I shake my head. "You don't need to give me compliments when I almost got you killed."

"Nah, Lennox wouldn't have killed me. He's just showing me I have a lot to learn to do my part in keeping you safe. I'll practice and do better next time," Kit says.

I frown. "No, you—"

"I'll keep practicing and getting stronger. I won't fail you, Rialta. I love you. I'm the weak link, but I won't let my weakness hurt you."

"You're not the weak link." I kiss his forehead. "And you have nothing to prove. I just want you to be able to protect yourself. But these guys will ensure that you're safe, I promise."

I look up at Hayes, who doesn't seem bothered that I've added Kit to the list of people he needs to protect. Gage just nods, assuming Kit was always going to be included. But then I glare at Lennox, and he simply stands there staring at me. He won't let me boss him around. It's something I'm going to have to take up with him later, and I plan on it.

I shoot daggers in Lennox's direction for one more second, before turning all of my attention back to Kit. "Do you want to try sitting up?"

He nods, and Hayes and I gently help him sit up. Blood starts streaming down his nose, and I'm afraid it's broken. Gage tosses us a rag to hold to Kit's nose, and a few minutes later, we help him stand up.

Lennox does nothing. He doesn't apologize; he doesn't offer to help—nothing.

I'm raging.

But I need to focus on Kit.

"Can you walk?"

"I feel fine, honest. My head hurts a little, along with my nose, but otherwise, I'm fine. I'm not on the verge of death, bug."

I force a smile, although the situation is anything but fine.

"We're going next door, so I can clean Kit up before he has to leave for work. Leave us alone, all of you," I say, not waiting for them to approve.

I lead Kit to Lennox's apartment.

"Wow, it's like his personality was turned into an apartment," Kit says after looking around the space.

"Yea, the apartment is somehow grumpy, arrogant, and an asshole all at once."

I take his hand and gently lead him up the stairs to the bathroom.

I sit him down on the closed toilet lid and start running water in the sink. I wet a clean washcloth and wipe the blood away to reveal a nasty bruise forming under his eye.

I wince, but he doesn't.

"That has to hurt," I say.

He shakes his head. "Stop trying to make me leave you. I can't. I love you, bug."

I smile at the nickname that always melts me a little. He used to tease me that I was like a bug he couldn't get rid of. Now he's happy I kept following him around all those years.

"I just don't like seeing you hurt or risking your life. It's not fair," I say.

"No, it's not. But you live your life with a risk of dying all the time. That's not fair, either. I'll do whatever it takes to be with you."

I frown and rest my forehead against his. "I can't lose you. I'd give you up before I let anyone hurt you."

"I know, which is why I love you. You're so selfless. You're too good to me."

"I can't be with you. I can't ever marry you. I can't have your kids. I can't ever truly be with you." A sob catches in my throat as hopelessness overwhelms me.

"Don't give up so quickly, bug. You don't know what our future holds." He runs his finger over my rings. "I don't care that you're married to that asshole. There's still time to figure a way out of this mess. Maybe if I prove I'm strong enough, your father will let me marry you eventually after I get rid of Lennox."

I shake my head. "You'd have to do the job. You'd have to be a mob boss, and no matter how strong you become, you could never do it. You're not a sadist who likes to kill for fun."

He sighs. "We'll figure this out."

And then he grabbed my thighs and lifted me up after standing.

I squeal. "Kit, what are you doing? You need to rest, not be lifting me."

"What I need to be doing is giving you an orgasm."

"What?"

"I owe you an orgasm. Last time, you didn't come. You faked it."

I blush. "I didn't—"

"You did."

I snap my mouth shut, embarrassed. "I'm sorry."

"No, I'm sorry. I should have made you come."

"We were a little busy trying to stay alive."

"We have time now." He winks at me and then carries me to the bed, plopping me down on my back in the pile of pillows and covers.

"Kit," I try to protest, but he's already spread my legs and buried his face between them. The second his lips touch my inner thigh, I stop protesting—I need this. I need the release and to feel connected to him. And if he thinks he's well enough for this, *then who am I to argue?*

He licks hungrily up my leg, until he reaches the edge of the black briefs I'm wearing. I'm not sure what he thinks about me wearing another man's underwear. I don't know if he believes me when I say there is nothing between me and Lennox. I'm only wearing them because I have no clothes here.

Kit doesn't ask. He doesn't have to—he trusts me.

His teeth sink into the thin material, and I hear a rip. I arch my back, so I can see him become feral and possessive as he tears the underwear from my body.

I pant at the sight of his hungry look before spreading my legs wider and dipping his head between my seams.

I let out a low groan as his tongue licks up my slit and to my clit. Any and all thoughts shoot out of my head as his tongue moves over me. His firm hands keep me spread, and he growls—claiming me as his.

In this moment, I am his.

It doesn't matter who I'm married to—whose ring I wear. It doesn't even matter if I carry Lennox's child. I'm Kit's. I'm his love, and he's mine.

And he's showing me exactly how much nothing else matters. Our love will endure.

I writhe beneath him as his expert tongue flicks over my sensitive nub. I feel my cheeks heating, my body trembling, and the tingling in my core building.

"I love you, bug," Kit says, his words vibrating through me, intensifying the feeling.

"I love you, too."

I grab his head as I feel him move faster, and I move closer to the brink of coming.

His hand goes over mine, and I feel him touch my wedding and engagement rings. He flicks it around and squeezes my hand hard, trying to grind the rings off my finger. Rings I forgot I was even wearing. Rings I should have taken off before I let him bring me pleasure.

"You're mine," he growls.

I gasp as his teeth nip at my clit, sending intense waves through my body.

"Say it," he commands.

"I'm yours," I whimper.

Satisfied, his tongue pushes me over the edge.

Waves of emotion slam through me like a hurricane. My head spins with the intensity, and tears well in my eyes as I feel myself being torn by our predicament. *How can our love survive this? How can I best protect Kit?*

I grab Kit's shirt and pull him to me as I kiss him hard. I can taste my sweet juices on his lips as I kiss him.

"I'm sorry," I whisper, even though I know none of this is my fault. But it is my fault for letting him fall in love with me, knowing that my life wasn't mine. My heart was never free to give. I knew this would always end tragically like Romeo and Juliet.

He shakes his head and kisses me again. "Don't ever be sorry. Falling in love with you will never be a mistake."

I disagree, but don't say it. I don't say that his life is more important than loving me.

"My turn," I say, but Kit just kisses me again.

"I have to go to work."

I frown. "But you're a mess. You need to be monitored for signs of a concussion. You can't go to work."

"I'll be fine, but I'll text you every hour, so you don't worry."

"Kit, I—"

"I'll be fine, bug. Don't worry about me."

He kisses me again, and I have no choice but to surrender. If he's going to keep being with me, then he'll do far riskier things in his life than this.

"We need to talk more," I say.

"I know, and we will, but you won't change my mind. And neither will your husband, even if he punches me and breaks my nose every day. Nothing will keep me away from you. I love you, bug. Don't doubt that."

"I don't."

"Good."

He kisses me one more time and then jogs down the stairs and out the door, leaving me tingling and my muscles limp after what just happened. I lie back on the bed, basking in my post-orgasm high and the sweet moment we shared—pretending I can hold onto this feeling forever.

But I need to deal with Lennox, and the longer I lay here, the angrier I get.

I stand up and stomp downstairs, ready to head next door to give Lennox a piece of my mind. When my feet hit the last step, I hear him.

I whip my head toward the kitchen, where he's pouring himself a glass of whiskey.

"What are you doing here?" I snap, stomping toward him.

"This is my apartment." Lennox sips his whiskey while standing in jeans and a dark grey shirt. His hair is messily poured over one side of his head, and he has a serious, concerned look on his face—always scowling and intense.

"And I told you to wait next door," I say through gritted teeth.

"And I don't take orders from you."

I narrow my eyes, trying to figure out the best way to hurt him. "How long have you been here?"

"Do you mean how much did I overhear?" He raises his eyebrows, and I blush, knowing he heard everything.

"I was here long enough to hear Kit go all cave-man possessive and give you a pathetic excuse for a climax in my bed."

"It wasn't pathetic—that release was incredible."

He shrugs. "It seemed mildly pleasant from where I was standing."

"How would you know what a mind-blowing orgasm sounds like? I doubt you've ever gotten a woman off before. You're too selfish and serious to go down on any woman."

His eyes intensify, and his teeth rake over his bottom lip. A heated smolder drags up and down my body. Suddenly, my legs feel weak like jello, my insides stir to life, and my nipples harden. He's a fucking magician that can control my body without touching me.

It can't be possible. I must still be turned on from Kit.

I fold my arms across my chest, realizing how naked I am. I'm still just wearing Lennox's shirt, and I'm no longer wearing any underwear. Under Lennox's stare, it feels like I'm wearing nothing at all.

"Would you like me to try? I could show you what a real orgasm feels like." He leans against the counter casually, like he just offered to make me the best cup of coffee, not touch me in the most intimate of ways.

Sex is nothing to him. He's probably fucked enough women that fucking is the same as talking to him.

"No, I don't want you to try. I know you wouldn't be any good."

"When I win the bet, and you beg me to fuck you, you'll realize what you've been missing."

I'm angry, but the tiniest of smiles slips onto my face. He's no longer sulking. He's back to the bickering, grumpy flirtatious man I knew before we got married. The man I can go toe to toe against. The man I can beat, unlike the dark savage from last night with too many demons to have a chance at winning.

"If you ever punch Kit again or hurt a hair on his head, I'll kill you. I don't care what my father, or anyone else, thinks. I'll deal with the consequences. You won't hurt him again. In fact, you'll protect him. That's what I've added to our arrangement in order for me to be a dutiful wife."

"You can't save him." He looks sad as he says it, like he's sharing a piece of his own soul with me as he speaks.

"What? Of course I—"

"You can't. No matter what you try. He'll never be safe. You know that. The only way is to give him up completely."

I frown. "You're just trying to win your stupid bet."

He shrugs. "Maybe. Or maybe I just have experience in this. Trust me."

He grabs his whiskey and heads toward the living room. "Also, I got your clothes for a reason, so you don't have to keep wearing *mine*."

I stomp over to him, about to give him another piece of my mind, but I decide I should put on my own clothes before I fight with Lennox more. I don't know why I keep wearing his except to piss him off.

Trust me, he says.

I don't trust him.

CHAPTER 20

Lennox

I SULK for the next three days and barely see Rialta. She's not a morning person, so it's easy to slip out of the apartment before she even wakes up. But I'm tired of sleeping on the couch. If this is going to continue, then I at least need to buy a better couch that converts into a bed or something.

Rialta spends most of her days with Hayes. He teaches her how to fight and cook, while Gage and I spend our days looking for the man who wants to kill Rialta. It would be so much easier if we found him. Then all of this game of trying to make Rialta love me could be over. I'd become Corsi's successor instead of inching closer to my death.

I try to tell myself the main reason I've been avoiding Rialta is because I'm focused on my work, and I'm not ready to have any more conversations with her about our wedding night. In reality, I can't get the sound of Kit licking her in my bed out of my head. It was absolute torture listening to him elicit such delicious sounds from her mouth.

In. My. Bed.

The balls on that boy are solid as steel to have done that. Maybe I underestimated him. *How am I going to make*

Rialta grow real feelings for me if there's nothing wrong with the man she's currently in love with? And he has the advantage of not having killed an innocent man in front of her.

"Should we take dinner to our apartment? Lennox doesn't have a table," Gage says, standing next to me at the bar of my kitchen, while Hayes and Rialta finish preparing dinner.

"No, let's eat on the couch," Rialta says.

I eye her suspiciously. I don't know what it is about my apartment that draws her in, but she feels more comfortable here than anywhere else. Works for me since I feel the same, but I don't know why it's the case for her.

The guys don't argue. Everyone grabs a plate and a glass of wine, and then we all find a spot on the sectional. Hayes and Gage sit next to each other. Rialta sits on the opposite end. As much as I want to sit as far away from Rialta as possible, I force myself to sit so that my thigh brushes against hers.

She notices and tries to squirm away from me into the armrest, but there's not enough room. Our thighs touch, and our arms brush against each other every time either of us moves.

We all eat silently, enjoying the dinner Hayes and Rialta made. But Hayes always has to be an instigator with rude comments.

"So, how are you two getting along?" he says with a smirk.

"Fine," I say at the same time Rialta says, "If we don't kill each other within the month, it will be a miracle."

I frown, looking in her direction. "What? It's the truth. You want to kill me. And you would have already, if you could still take over Vincent's job with me dead." She elbows me hard, trying to give herself breathing room.

I don't budge. She's going to have to fight harder than

that to get rid of me. I'm a stubborn man, and I intend on getting everything I want.

Instead of moving, I drape my arm around her shoulders, my hand resting against the sensitive spot on the back of her bicep.

"That's not what I want to do to you. I'd much rather tie you up and spank that pretty ass of yours again before slamming my cock deep in that tight cunt," I tease.

Rialta doesn't blush or so much as blink at my dirty talk. I frown.

"What are you doing? Do you really think putting your arm around me is going to have me weak at the knees, begging for you to kiss me or something?" Rialta says with amusement in her eyes, completely ignoring my comment.

Hayes snickers, and Gage tries to hide his own smile as he shovels in a mouthful of food.

"No, I don't think any such thing." She can pretend that we don't share any physical attraction all she wants, but I can feel her shiver ever so slightly beneath my touch. She can't help her body's reaction to me.

I'm about to push things further when an alert goes off on Gage's phone. He immediately jumps to attention, with Hayes catching on a second later. They both whip their guns out and race out the door.

I don't have time to explain to Rialta what's going on, and I know she's going to be pissed at me instead of thanking me later, but at least she'll be alive to yell at me. I scoop her in my arms, and I'm up the loft stairs in two seconds.

My bedroom has a small walk-in closet that I push inside and rush to the back, where we've created a small safe room. I enter the door code quickly, thrust it open, and push us both inside. The metal door slams shut behind us, cloaking the safe room in darkness.

I grab my gun and hold it at my side, as we stand pressed against each other face to face, breath to breath, chest to chest. Our breaths are fast and erratic. I have no idea what the threat is or whether Gage and Hayes are going to survive it. As I listen to her quick breaths, I suddenly realize I'm actually worried about her.

Rialta drives me absolutely crazy. She's far too carefree, reckless, and cavalier with her own life. But she doesn't deserve to die.

I keep my phone in my hand, waiting for a signal from Gage that everything is safe again. My gun is still in the other, ready to attack if the apartment is breached.

Rialta doesn't ask any questions, doesn't doubt that her life is in danger once again. But suddenly, I hear her breathing slow, and then I feel her hand on my chest.

"What?" I ask.

She doesn't speak. She just keeps her hand over my heart, and I feel her calming, steadying presence.

I start breathing with her, slowing my tempo to match hers until my heart is calm. I've never had someone touch me like that, never had someone calm me.

My heart skips a beat at the thought of this woman. I've never wanted to kiss someone or hold someone so much in my life. It has to be our proximity to each other in this cramped safe room that's doing it.

I'm always the calm, steady one, the one who isn't flustered. But I couldn't hide my true self from her in a space like this. She felt the anxiety and fear flowing through me, and she relaxed me.

I don't know why she did it. And I don't know how she's able to be so serene herself when faced with death so frequently for such a young woman.

My phone buzzes in my hand, the light from the phone

lighting up our faces as we stare intently into each other's eyes. I glance down.

"It's safe. Gage says it was a false alarm."

Her lips part, and her tongue rubs over her bottom lip. I very much want to taste that lip.

I grind my teeth together, biting my own tongue in the process, and I wince.

"Are you okay?" she asks with full sincerity.

"Yes," I growl back, mad at myself for not keeping my horny feelings under wraps for this woman.

I open the door, and we spill out without a word, a thank you, anything to each other.

She heads straight to the bathroom. I head downstairs to clean up the food and wine, knowing no one is going to feel like eating after what just happened.

Gage comes in while I'm cleaning up. "Someone is playing games with us."

"What do you mean?"

He holds out the phone and shows a loop of men entering our apartment building with guns.

"No one entered the building. This is fake. It didn't really happen."

I frown. "Why would someone do that?"

"I don't know. To scare us. To keep us on edge."

"Be on guard tonight."

"I always am," Gage says before leaving.

I throw the last of the dishes into the dishwasher, and then I head upstairs, where Rialta has already climbed into bed.

After removing my shirt and placing my gun on the nightstand, I start removing my jeans.

"What are you doing?" Rialta asks, looking up from her phone.

"Getting ready for bed."

"You can do that downstairs."

I shake my head. "I'm not leaving you alone, not after what happened just now. And I haven't forgotten you're liable to sneak out in the middle of the night. I want a good night's sleep for once."

"You won't get a good night's sleep next to me. Sleep on the floor."

"No." I throw the covers back after I'm down to my briefs and climb into bed next to her.

"If we are going to stay in this apartment, then I want to sleep in my own bed again. I'm not going to sleep on the couch forever."

There is no way I'm letting her sleep by herself again. It's too risky. The only way I'll get any sleep is next to her in bed, even if she drives me absolutely crazy. If she's kidnapped or dead, this will all be for nothing.

"I snore," she says.

I shrug, pulling the covers up. "I'll wear some earplugs if it bothers me."

"I roll around a lot in my sleep."

"You'll learn to roll around on just one side."

"I fart a lot. I smell horrible. You won't be able to stand it."

I chuckle. "So do I."

There's a hint of a smile on her face before I turn off the lamp. But once the darkness descends, we are both quiet. We don't speak, but we're doing the same thing—listening for any signs of monsters in the night while ensuring that neither of us develops any feelings for the other.

CHAPTER 21

Lennox

"DAMN, you really do fart a lot in your sleep," I say as a morning greeting.

She rolls over toward me and shoves her face into the pillow, hiding her embarrassment. I suspect it has more to do with the moaning and writhing she was doing in her sleep this morning than any smell. She doesn't smell; I'm just trying to make her smile and see there's no reason to be embarrassed. I'm sure her sex dream this morning was about Kit, her supposed true love.

She throws her pillow at my head. "You should sleep on the ground tonight, so you don't have to smell my farts."

"Just downstairs? People walking by in the hallway are passing out from your stink."

"They aren't that bad."

With a disgusted face, I jump out of bed and beat her to the bathroom, shutting the door in her face.

She slams her hand on the door a moment later. "Dammit, Lennox! I really have to pee."

I smirk, taking my sweet time.

When I come out, she's somehow finished all the coffee

in the apartment, as well as Gage and Hayes's coffee stash next door.

I use all of the hot water showering.

She hides all of the food except for some kimchi and a bottle of ketchup.

I accidentally break her phone charger, so her phone dies by mid-afternoon.

She gets red wine all over my favorite sweatshirt.

This is how our day goes—little battles back and forth to avoid having any real conversations or feelings, until Rialta gets fed up enough to ask for what she really wants.

"I'm going to see Kit tonight. What security do you want me to bring with me?" Rialta says as soon as I return from an early evening run to find her pacing my living room.

"No," is all I say as I walk in and head straight to my bar, needing a stiff drink to handle her tonight.

"Um, you don't get to tell me no. I'm a grown woman who can make my own decisions," she says, hovering over me as I pour myself a scotch.

I squeeze my eyes shut, wishing that would shut everything out, but it just makes the visions worse. They keep coming, flooding my head—over and over and over again—images of her.

Of her smile.

Of her laugh.

Of her dying.

Of history repeating itself.

I try to take a deep breath, knowing I need to breathe, to meditate, to medicate—something to get rid of the panic that keeps rising inside of me, but I can't.

"No," I say again, this time rougher than before. I can't get anything else out. I can't explain to her that I'm having a panic attack, that I feel déjà vu every time I'm with her. The thought of her leaving my sight right now and risking her life is not something I can bear in this moment.

"I'm going. Send Hayes or Gage, but I'm going to see Kit tonight."

"No." I grab her wrist, snagging her hand where she's wearing my engagement and wedding rings. I'm breathing uncontrollably. One second I'm sucking in too much air too fast; the next, I'm barely taking in enough to remain standing.

"Lennox?" Rialta's face goes white, finally noticing my state.

I squeeze my eyes shut tighter, trying to make it stop. My hands ball at my sides, and sweat pours down my face.

Death—all I see is death coming. Again.

"Lennox," her voice is soft and distant.

I'm not going to be enough.

I'm going to fail.

I'm going to die before I succeed, just like before.

And Rialta is going to die, too, because I'm the only man who can protect her.

I feel my legs giving out.

At least I don't love Rialta like I loved her. I don't even like her. I'm just not sure she deserves to die because of me.

I fall to the floor, the world spinning.

Breathe.

Her voice echoes in my head.

I want to die to stop the pain.

But I can't.

I have to finish what I started.

I can't fail.

Suddenly I feel warm lips on mine, followed by a hot breath shuddering through my lungs.

At first, I fight the air, not wanting it to enter my body. *Don't bring me back to life, just let the anxiety take me away.*

But the breath is insistent on ensuring I live. It fills me again and again. And then I feel more—the soft lips pressing against mine and a tongue massaging mine. My body warms and comes alive the longer her lips are on mine.

Her hand strokes my hair while another presses gently against my chest. It's reassuring she cares enough to check if I'm still alive.

I've had plenty of panic attacks—plenty of times my anxiety has crippled me. At night there have also been plenty of times my nightmares took hold, triggering the trauma of my past. But never have I had someone help me through it.

Ever so slowly, the anxiety slithers out of my body, and the pain in my chest lessens. The trauma is still there—it will always be there—but her lips give me something to focus on besides the darkness.

I squint, watching her try to breathe life into me. To me, it feels more like a desperate kiss than a mere supply of oxygen. I enjoy the feeling a second longer than I should before finally opening my eyes.

"Thank god!" She falls back on her heels, kneeling as she watches me closely. "Do I need to call an ambulance? Did you have a heart attack or something?"

"No," I say gently.

"Is that all you can say to me?" she says with annoyance.

I shake my head, needing a second. "It wasn't a heart attack."

"Then, what was it?"

I look at her and know someday, I'll reveal my darkest secret. Someday she'll know my entire truth, but that day isn't today. It's not the right time.

"I had too much to drink, and I blacked out."

Disappointment hangs in her dark orbs as she stares at me. "Fine, don't tell me. Gage will stay with you, and Hayes can go with me to meet Kit."

"No."

She rolls her eyes. "We're not back to that."

"I want to change our arrangement."

"I'm not giving him up." She stands up abruptly.

"You are." I follow suit and rise to my feet.

"No, I'm not. We had an agreement."

"And I had an agreement with Vincent, but that changed..."

She goes quiet. "I can't give him up."

"I'm not risking my life for puppy love."

"It's not puppy love."

"Give Kit up."

"No."

"Do you love him?"

"Yes, with everything in my body."

I nod. "Then, if you truly love him, this will make you feel nothing." I grab her neck and kiss her. Not the tame lip touching she was doing before—this kiss is a take no prisoners kind of kiss. I don't give her time to react. My tongue is deep in her mouth as soon as my lips land on hers. My thumbs caress her jawline, and my fingers tangle in her hair.

My goal is simple—fuck with her mind and make her realize she doesn't love him. I'm about to play dirty as far as our bet is concerned. But it isn't about the bet—it's about her father. I'll die if I fail to meet either of his challenges.

And I'm doomed to fail. I'll never be able to find and stop the man who hunts her, and I'll never fall in love with her. My only hope is to make her fall in love with me—she can save me.

This kiss is a desperate attempt at making her feel anything for me. I'm not charming. I'm not a nice man. She's seen the shadows of my darkness even if she hasn't seen the depth of it yet. My only hope is to make her see that she doesn't love Kit and that I could make her happy. He's a boy; I'm a man.

She shoves me hard.

"You're not a monster. Stop acting like one."

Quickly, I see how I affected her. She enjoyed that kiss. She enjoys being in my arms even if it confuses her.

"When you fuck him tonight, don't think of me," I say with a smug expression, knowing full well she will. And I'm going to need a boxing session with Gage tonight to survive the thought of Kit being inside her.

Rialta

I STRADDLE KIT—RIDDING his thick cock as he grins up at me. I smile back weakly, trying my best to stay in the present. All of my efforts are going into staying completely focused on Kit and not even thinking about anything, or anyone, else.

A flash of blue eyes replaces Kit's green ones. I shake my head, trying to make them go away.

"You okay?" Kit asks.

"Hmmm, this feels so good."

"Yea, it does." He thrusts upward, filling me completely.

I moan and close my eyes—big mistake.

Lennox's smirk and words play in my head—*when you fuck him tonight, don't think of me.*

Dammit.

Damn him.

It's just because I've been spending so much time with Lennox lately, and so much of my mind is spent thinking about our marriage and what happened on our wedding night. It's not because I enjoyed his kiss or his smug expression. It's just the stress of my situation that puts him in my thoughts constantly.

It's not fair to Kit.

I take a deep breath and banish the images, returning to the present.

It does feel good to be riding him. Him buried deep inside me, my clit rubbing against his hard lower stomach, his hands twirling my nipples into peaks—everything is on track for an epic climax.

But I'm not going to come. I'll be lucky if I can fake a convincing orgasm.

I should talk to Kit, but I don't even know where to start. Being present with him for the rest of this is a start.

Suddenly, Kit's bedroom door flies open. Hayes is covering his eyes with a hand.

"I'm sorry. Finish quickly; we have to go—now."

I frown. "What's happened?" I'm already climbing off Kit, and he's cursing his missed opportunity for release. At least I won't have to pretend like he could satisfy me. I can get my act together and try again after dealing with whatever drama Hayes is bringing.

Hayes peeks behind his hands and sees me pulling my shirt back on. He glances away again as he says, "It's Corsi business."

I don't know what that means except that it's something he doesn't want to explain in front of Kit.

I pull on my pants as Kit continues to lie naked on his bed.

"Give us a minute," I tell Hayes.

"One minute," he says before closing the door behind him.

"I'm so sorry," I say as I climb back up the bed and straddle him again, this time fully clothed. I wrap my arms around his neck and stare deeply into his eyes.

"It's okay. It's not your fault. It won't always be like this. Someday, we'll find a way out. For now, this is enough. I get to have you almost every night. I get to kiss you, to love you.

"And even though you are technically married to that son of a bitch, and you have responsibilities you have to attend to tonight, I don't have to worry about sharing you—not really. I'm the only one who gets to kiss you." He leans in and kisses me tenderly. "And I'm the only one who gets to fuck you."

I swallow down a lump in my throat. I haven't told him everything that has happened between Lennox and me. To be honest, I don't even know the whole truth of what has happened or how Lennox feels. And I decide I'm not going to share anything with Kit until I understand myself. There is no point in discussing it until then. And I don't have time to talk to him about it now anyway.

"I love you. I'll text you later when I can," I say, kissing him one more time.

He smiles. "I love you too, bug."

I offer him a small smile before heading out and finding Hayes. He doesn't speak as we leave Kit's apartment or as we walk to the car.

Hayes starts driving. "You should talk to Kit."

I frown. "Eavesdropping, were you? I thought you said you'd put your AirPods in and not listen to us."

Hayes grins. "What fun is that?"

I glare at Hayes. "If you're going to be my main security when I visit Kit, you can't listen to us fuck."

He frowns. "I need to listen for any signs of an intruder."

"Find a way to do it without listening to us."

"Fine, I'll come up with something. But that doesn't change the fact that you should talk to Kit. It's not fair to him."

I sigh. "I know, but none of this is fair to me either."

Hayes snaps his mouth shut and doesn't say anything the rest of the drive to Vincent's condo. And I don't ask why we're going there, assuming that's where we're headed.

I spot Lennox's car in the parking garage. Hayes and I step out of our car as Lennox and Gage get out of theirs.

They both look serious and intense. I try to read the situation, but I come up empty.

Lennox grabs my hand like we hold each other's hands all the time. But that one motion tells me all I need to know —we need to put on a united front.

We enter Vincent's floor and head to the conference room to find a dozen of Vincent's high-ranking men are gathered. I'm the only female in the room, so I'm not sure what I'm doing here.

Everyone stares at Lennox and me as we walk in. It's expected every time I walk into a room, but this time it feels different. These men heard what happened on our wedding night. They heard us fighting, me pleading. They heard what they thought was Lennox forcing himself on me.

Most of the men look at me with a smug expression of near ownership—it's disgusting. They look pleased to think Lennox has finally put me in my place. I will no longer bring Vincent or any of the Corsi men any problems from now on. I've been tamed.

They don't know the truth.

I stand tall and proud—trying to look as strong as River would be in this situation. I don't cower.

I try to pull my hand loose from Lennox's grip, not wanting to look like he controls me, but he holds on tighter, not letting me go.

As we walk to our chairs at the far end of the table next to Vincent, a hand reaches out and grabs my ass.

"When you're finished with her, we'd all like like a turn," the man says.

My heart stops.

I don't think Vincent would ever let that happen, but it's no longer his decision—it's Lennox's. And if he thinks it will get him better standing with these men, I'm not sure the lengths Lennox would go to get more power.

Lennox stops, forcing me to come to a halt.

The fury splashed on Lennox's face is stronger than I've ever seen it.

He turns and grabs the man's hand, while never letting go of mine. The audible sounds of hand bones cracking precede the man's howl of pain.

"Do. Not. Touch. My. Wife," Lennox demands. He looks around the room. "That goes for all of you. Touch her, and I'll kill you. I don't care who you are."

And then Lennox punches the man so hard his unconscious head slams against the conference table in a thud.

The room is silent.

No one speaks.

I look to Vincent, who gives a tight smile in Lennox's direction. It's what Vincent would have done in the situation.

Lennox leads us to our chairs, and we sit, while Hayes and Gage stand behind us like bodyguards.

Vincent starts. "Edoardo called this emergency meeting, so he has the floor." Vincent gives him an annoyed look. I'm guessing this better be important, or Edoardo will probably end up dead on the floor.

Lennox continues to grip my hand, but he doesn't look or speak to me. He's eagerly staring at Edoardo to get on with it.

"I'll get right to the point. We are being infiltrated. An enemy is trying to find our weaknesses, and I'm not sure if

Lennox is up for the job of keeping Rialta and the Corsi line safe," Edoardo says.

Lennox looks like he's going to kill Edoardo—so does Vincent.

"I assume you have some kind of evidence for your claims?" Vincent asks.

Edoardo slides a picture to Vincent. He studies it for a second, and then slides it toward Lennox and me.

I force myself not to react, but my heart rate takes off like a rocket. It's a picture of Kit and me kissing outside his apartment. It's grainy, so it's hard to make out who the man is, but it's us embracing and kissing.

"This photo was taken earlier this evening. Either Rialta was kidnapped tonight, and we weren't all informed, or Lennox has been loaning her out before an heir has been produced. Either way, it risks the Corsi line."

Shit.

I was so stupid. The one thing Lennox required of me was to be discreet. I could keep Kit as long as he was the only one who knew about it. I fucked up by being seen with him.

And now, I have no idea how we are going to get out of this mess.

Lennox could end up dead because of me, and so could Kit. I don't know how to save either of them.

Hayes peers over my shoulder.

"Sorry, um, but that's a picture of me," Hayes says suddenly.

All eyes snap to him.

"I'm used to getting to share Lennox's girls or at least getting a taste. I wasn't thinking when I kissed her." Hayes takes off his glasses and lifts his shirt to reveal multiple deep bruises I didn't notice before. "Lennox ensured I paid the price for it, and I won't be making that mistake again."

Lennox gives Hayes the tightest of nods.

Hayes has saved us. He was there tonight, so if anyone looks into it further, it will make sense. He's currently wearing a dark hoodie similar to what Kit was wearing in the photo. And the hood is up, so it's impossible to tell who I'm kissing.

Lennox glares at Edoardo. "As you can see, I have everything under control. Rialta is safe and *mine*. And you'll have your Corsi heir within the year. It's late. Everyone is dismissed. And next time you call an emergency meeting late at night, make sure it is actually an emergency."

He yanks me up, and we all walk out of the room before anyone can question his authority.

But I know I fucked up.

My two worlds are already starting to clash. It wouldn't take much digging for someone motivated enough to find the truth and kill Kit, no questions asked. I know what I have to do, but it's going to break me.

CHAPTER 23

Lennox

HAYES SAVED US.

He's not usually that quick-witted, but I'm going to have to find a way to thank him. We all are. If it wasn't for him, we'd all be dead.

Rialta would have been the only one to survive, but she'd be forced to marry someone far crueler than me. It would be a man who would take what he wanted from her until he's bled her of everything worth living. She'd be as good as dead.

We all owe him our lives.

I don't let go of Rialta's hand until I've led her to the door of my car. I don't leave her side until she's climbed in and buckled her seatbelt.

Then I turn to Hayes and Gage, who are climbing into Hayes's car.

"Thank you," I say to Hayes, knowing it's not enough.

He shakes his head. "We've all saved each other plenty of times. You'd all do the same for me. Besides, my neck was on the line too."

I nod and look to Gage, who is looking tired and grateful.

And then we all climb into our cars. I know they will follow closely in case we are followed or attacked on the way home.

As I start driving, I try to keep my thoughts on the road, but it's impossible for my mind not to wander to that man touching Rialta—trying to violate her. My mind can't not think about all of those men's filthy, disgusting thoughts wanting to rape her.

I want to squeeze my eyes shut to block them out, but I can't. I have to keep my eyes on the road, but I might as well be watching a movie of their desires. I can see so clearly how they'd strip her, beat her, force her open, and fuck her against her will.

"I'm sorry I was reckless with Kit," says Rialta, her voice reminding me of where I am.

My hands tighten on the steering wheel, and I blink hard. I push the thoughts of the Corsi men away, but they're replaced just as quickly with images of her and Kit last night. Them fucking in his bed fills my vision, not caring who they hurt or who dies so they can carry on pretending their love is story is one of epic proportions. When actually, if they were to get married, they'd be divorced within five years.

There is nothing special about their love story. Their love is built on living next door to each other for years and an infatuation with each other. It wouldn't even surprise me if Kit likes this arrangement. He gets to fuck her but doesn't have to live with her. Doesn't have to spend his money on her. Doesn't have to raise any kids. And he can easily cheat without her being upset with him because she's married to me. It's a win-win situation for him.

"Sorry isn't enough," I finally reply.

"I know it's not."

"Do you? Do you understand what you risked tonight? Do you realize you could have gotten us all killed? Hayes, Gage, me, and Kit—we all could have died because of your mistake."

"I'm sorry. I never wanted to hurt anyone, and I definitely didn't want anyone to die because of me."

I park the car in my building garage and close my eyes, trying to block out my own darkness. I know how she feels. I've been in her shoes. People I've loved have died because of my mistakes. I just hope she learns from my mistakes before someone actually ends up dead.

"I need to see Kit."

"What?" I snap in her direction, convinced I must have heard her wrong. I'm hoping she's going to give him up eventually, or at least, lay low for a while before she sees him again. Later we can come up with a better plan for how and when they can see each other. I didn't think she'd run into his arms tonight.

"I'm going to see Kit—tonight."

I shake my head. "No, you're not."

She looks dead serious as she looks at me. "I'm going. We had a deal. I've played my part. And I'll continue to, but I need to see Kit."

Rage rises through my body, and any hope of me ever falling for her or truly caring for her goes out the window. I thought she was learning how to be selfless. I thought she was starting to care about all of us. But she's just a spoiled, selfish princess like I originally thought.

I won't let her bring everyone I care about down with her, even if she's content on getting everyone she loves killed.

I could drag her inside, lock her up until she comes to her senses.

Or...

"Go." I look her dead in the eyes. "But I'll not send my

men on a suicide mission. If you go to Kit, you go without protection."

Her eyes widen, but she doesn't back down. She walks out the car door, past Hayes and Gage, and then out of the garage.

"Should we follow her?" Gage asks.

"No."

I can't save her. She's on her own.

CHAPTER 24

Rialta

I KNOCK on River and Beckett's door gently, almost hoping they won't answer. But I don't really have another choice. I need somewhere safe to sleep tonight. I'm soaking wet and terrified and shaken from what I've lived through tonight.

I'm not going back to Lennox's, and I'm definitely not going to my father's. And Kit's not a choice, not anymore.

I'm sure they have the place monitored, so they probably saw me approach before I even knocked. Not two seconds later, Beckett is opening the door in his boxers with a scowl on his face.

Wordlessly, he opens the door and lets me in. I know he's annoyed with me, even after all we've been through together. The secrets we've shared and my part in ensuring he got to marry the love of his life don't make up for me risking his child's life with my antics.

He closes the door behind me. "Ri's asleep."

"I didn't come here to talk to her. I just came here for a safe place to sleep. I'll get up and leave before she wakes up, so she won't know I was here."

He frowns. "What happened?"

I raise an eyebrow, shocked Lennox didn't call to inform them how reckless I was. I guess I truly am on my own.

"I did something stupid, as usual."

Beckett narrows his eyes, considering pulling more information from me. "You can sleep in the guest room. Let me know if you need anything."

"Thanks, I'm sure I'll manage for tonight."

I start walking toward the bedroom.

"And Rialta..."

I turn. "Yes?"

"You didn't do anything stupid. I know you—you have a big heart. Too big, actually. You deserve happiness and fun, and everything you want in life. Don't apologize or feel guilty for going after what you want. It's not stupid."

I nod, disagreeing, but it's late, and Beckett needs to go to bed.

I head into the guest bedroom. I should strip out of my wet clothes at least, but I'm too tired. I don't even bother to turn on the light or pull down the covers on the bed. I just collapse on top, knowing I won't sleep as I contemplate my next move.

Tears fall hard down my face. I've already made my decision. I put the first steps of that plan in motion tonight; tomorrow, I'll do the rest. I sob, hoping the despair will eventually pull me into sleep's darkness.

It never does.

———

Alone in the hallway, I stand in front of Lennox's door as my heart races. He's going to be pissed, and I have no idea what I'm going to say to him. But I can't make myself open the door to face him.

Suddenly, I hear yelling and then something breaking. I jump and push inside, needing to see what's going on.

My eyes widen, and my mouth gapes as I take in the scene.

Hayes is lying on his back on the couch with Gage and Lennox over him. Gage is holding him down, and Lennox is doing something to his shoulder. The apartment is in complete disarray. The floor is littered with pillows, broken glass, and bullet shell casings.

I race over to Hayes from the back side of the couch. I open my mouth to ask what happened, but then I see the blood—on all of them.

Hayes has the most blood on him, with it pouring out of his lower abdomen. The fact that he's the one doing the moaning on the couch and the other two are working over him tells me he's the one I should be concerned about at the moment.

"Fuck, stop!" Hayes yells as Lennox digs into the wound.

Lennox ignores him and definitely doesn't stop.

Hayes thrashes, while Gage tries to hold him down the best he can, panic-ridden on his face.

I grab Hayes's hand. "Hayes, look at me."

He does. "Shit, you look like hell," he says.

His hand squeezes mine hard as his arm trembles. I hold him steady, ignoring the cramping in my own hand. Whatever is wrong with him is serious, but at least he hasn't passed out—I tell myself that has to be a good thing. As long as Hayes is breathing and making jokes, then he's going to be fine.

"You don't look much better," I smirk back at him as he tries to smile through the pain, but he can't.

His face goes white, and I look from Hayes to Gage, who notices as well. Lennox continues doing whatever he's doing, his hands moving quickly, and his focus entirely on attending to Hayes's wounds.

"Hayes, stay with me. Tell me about your latest date. I'm sure you take women on the best dates," I say.

He opens his mouth, but nothing comes out. No moans. No snide remarks. Nothing.

Fuck.

"Hayes," I say, my voice cracking as I gently smack his face.

He turns his head toward me, but that's all he can manage.

I lean toward him, not sure if my idea will help, but it can't hurt. It will either help or give him one moment of peace before he dies. I can give him that.

My lips brush against his—they're still warm.

"He needs blood," Lennox says grimly.

"We should call an ambulance. Neither of us is his blood type," says Gage.

"I can donate. I'm O positive," I say.

Lennox and Gage both look at me.

"Give him my blood." I run around to the other side of the couch, where Lennox has started gathering the transfusion equipment.

I roll up my sleeve and hold out my arm.

Lennox takes the needle, looking at me for a second. I can see his anger at me boiling in his eyes, even now.

"Do it," I say, before feeling the needle pierce my skin.

Lennox attaches another needle to Hayes, pushing my blood into him.

"Hayes is going to be okay," Gage says, putting his hand on my shoulder. "He's breathing, and Lennox is good at playing doctor. With your blood pumping through his veins, he'll be good as new."

I nod. There isn't much to do now except wait for the

blood to do its job. Now I can finally get some answers. "What happened?"

Lennox doesn't speak. He still won't look at me.

"We were attacked," Gage says.

"By who?"

Gage hesitates and then says, "Retribution Kings."

I gasp and examine Gage more closely. His face is bruised, and he has a bloodied lip. There's a large scrape on his bicep. His shirt is draped in what must be Hayes's blood.

I study Lennox next. He has a black eye, a deep cut on his thigh, and Hayes's blood on his shirt too.

I want to ask more, but I decide it's better if I don't.

Gage looks at the container my blood is going in before being transferred to Hayes. "That's enough."

Lennox hesitates but removes the needle from my arm before slapping a bandaid over the puncture. He probably wishes he could have drained me of all my blood.

We all kneel next to the couch, watching Hayes. Slowly, the color returns to his face, and his breathing improves.

"He needs rest. There's nothing any of us can do for him now except get him rest," Gage says.

"Where?" Lennox asks.

"There is no place that's safe, not anymore. Our apartment is as good as anywhere else."

"I'll help you move him," Lennox says, ignoring me.

I lean forward and kiss Hayes on the forehead before Gage and Lennox lift him. They gently carry him to their apartment down the hall, while I sink onto Lennox's couch, my face in my hands. If I had any tears left, I would let them fall now. But I have none.

I have nothing left.

I know Hayes will be okay—*this time.*

But what about the next?

For once, I did the right thing being gone. *If I was here, who would have ended up dead? What lengths would the guys have gone to to protect me? Whose blood would I have on my hands this time?*

"Hayes woke up when we moved him," Lennox says, standing in the doorway. I hadn't even heard him return.

I watch him study me for the first time. I know I look a mess. I'm still wearing my rain-soaked clothes and didn't bother combing my hair or removing my makeup this morning. As bad as I look, he looks worse. I don't know how he's standing and not passed out somewhere.

"Gage is giving him some narcotics, so he'll sleep. Hayes has a low pain tolerance and will talk our heads off if he doesn't sleep."

I smile at that.

"I'm glad he's going to be okay," I say.

Lennox nods—his silent way of saying thanks to you. It's the only kind moment I get from him before his mask of rage returns.

"I'm surprised you're back. The sex mustn't have been very good if you're able to walk this morning and you're back before noon."

I take a deep breath. Lennox has no idea about the decision I've made or what happened last night, but I don't correct him. I let him be angry and take it out on me—I deserve it.

I stand up, knowing I have to face him. I have to act before I lose my nerve.

"We should talk," I say.

"We have nothing left to say. You made it clear where your loyalties lie. I know you don't care about me, but I thought you cared about Hayes and Gage. I thought you wouldn't sentence them to death so you can frolic with that bastard."

"He is a bastard," I quickly reply.

Lennox snaps his head in my direction. His eyes hone in on me, unsure if he heard me correctly.

I take the moment to walk toward him and put a hand on his forearm.

He yanks his arm away as he gazes at me.

"What happened? Did Kit kick you to the curve after he realized his life was at stake?"

I swallow hard. "No." Tears suddenly reappear to stain my eyes. "I found him in bed with another woman."

Lennox snickers.

"It's not funny!" I snap, my voice breaking.

"I told you it wasn't real love. One of you would eventually hurt the other."

"You want to tell me you told me so? Then do it."

"I told you so."

"Asshole," I breathe.

"Never claimed to be anything different. Maybe you'll come to your senses now that he's out of your life and stop being so fucking reckless."

He starts to walk past me, but I brush my hand over his arm again. He growls like I've stabbed him instead of brushing his bare skin, colored with a dark tattoo and a smear of blood.

"Stop. Doing. That."

I shake my head. "Help me," I whisper.

"I've helped you enough. I'm tired of helping you. Maybe it's time *you* helped *me*."

"It will help you too."

He pauses, his eyes turning dark as he realizes what I'm talking about. I don't know how he's going to react. This is the worst time to push him, but if I don't do it now, I'll never do it.

He chuckles. "You can't be serious?"

I turn on my puppy dog eyes. "I am."

He shakes his head. "You're delusional if you think I'm going to touch you."

I grind my teeth together. This is hard enough; of course, he's not going to make it easier on me.

"You will. It's what you've wanted this entire time. We made a bet, and you want to win. You'll fuck me because I'm offering. You'll win your stupid bet. And you'll get everything you want—me included."

He cocks an eyebrow, and a wolfish grin spreads over his face. "You think I still want you after everything?"

"You do."

"Hmmm." His eyes peruse up and down my body. "What I see is a naive and heartbroken woman in desperate need of a shower, not a woman I want to fuck."

Jesus, he's going to milk this.

He's going to make me beg, going to make me turn him on. He's punishing me for what he perceives as my fault.

Fine, he wants to play games? Let's play games.

"I think you very much want to fuck me. You've wanted to since the first moment you laid eyes on me, back when you thought I was going to marry one of your best friends."

His jaw ticks.

I grin, knowing the truth is hitting him.

"All that changed last night when you left to run back to your boyfriend, knowing it risked our lives!"

I blink as the force of his words slaps me in the face. I could tell him the truth of what happened. He would realize why I had to go and that it was very much to protect everyone here, but I won't. I don't want him to know.

I need Lennox angry. I need him to *take*, not *give*, when he finally fucks me. That's the only way this is going to end—him fucking me until there is nothing left of Kit inside my heart. Until our marriage is cemented in every way that matters. Until the world knows I belong to Lennox Corsi.

But I intend to keep as much of my pride as possible, along with my heart. I don't have to like the man to fuck him.

I grab the hem of my shirt and yank it over my head. I know I don't look my best, but Lennox has eyes, and as much as he's good at hiding his emotions, I know he won't when he sees my bare skin. And if he does, then I'll know he truly no longer finds me attractive.

He forces himself to keep his eyes on mine, not daring to let them drift down to my naked breasts or smooth stomach.

We stare at each other as if the first to look away loses. *I'm tired of losing. Tonight, I get what I want.*

I smirk. "Your staring is telling."

"Fine, I'll look." His hungry gaze runs down my body, taking his sweet, sweet time down the curve of my breasts, along my hardened nipples, and then even lower, imagining what's beneath my jeans. His eyes then snap up.

"Happy? I'm a man, and when presented with a pair of boobs in front of my face, I get turned on."

"Do you now? Or is it *my* boobs?" I try to keep the heat in my body at bay, not letting on that I was even the least bit turned on by his stare. But I'm sure my cheeks are flushed.

I trace my hand over the swell of my breasts, watching him watch me.

"Don't flatter yourself. Any hot-blooded man would be turned on by a nice pair of boobs."

"So my boobs are nice?"

He rolls his eyes. "I'm not the least bit tempted. You only want me to fuck you so you can forget what that cheating asshole did to you. Maybe you need to suffer the consequences of your actions."

I frown.

"You'll get over the bastard soon enough. I've seen true love, and you didn't really love him."

"You can help me find out."

He shakes his head, scoffing. "I don't want to help you." He leans forward to speak against my ear, his hot breath tickling my sensitive skin. "But if I were to fuck you, you'd realize immediately the only thing you love is my dick."

I feel my ear redden, along with my cheeks. My nipples are so fucking hard they hurt. "I think fucking you would be plenty of punishment."

His eyes dilate, and his nostrils flare. He wants to prove me wrong. I'm so close to getting what I want.

But then he turns around and starts jogging up the stairs without a word.

I sigh.

Fuck, why can't he cooperate just this once?

I walk up the stairs a minute later and find him in the bathroom. His shirt is on the floor, and he's washing his face and arms in the sink.

I stare from the doorway. My tongue runs over my lower lip as I watch his abs rippling, his chest rising and falling sharply as he tends to his wounds. His tattoos curve over every sharp edge of his body.

He splashes water on his face and runs his hand through his hair, slicking it back.

I'm practically salivating, watching the water drip down his pecs and biceps. He knows exactly what he's doing, too —the same thing I did when I removed my own shirt. But it feels like he's winning.

He turns and faces me. "You're drooling."

I snap my mouth shut and roll my eyes.

He lets out a wicked laugh that echoes off the walls. "You're pathetic, you know that?"

"And you're cruel."

"Tell me something I don't know, Corsi."

I frown. "Corsi is my father; call me Rialta."

His eyes thin into devilish slits, and his grin spreads. He likes to piss me off.

"But I rather like calling you Corsi—you and he both share the same ruthlessness."

"I'm not as ruthless as you are, Corsi," I throw the name at him as well.

He frowns. "I'm not…"

"You are a Corsi now." I grin, liking to see his own medicine thrown back at him. I know if he was any other guy, I would be putting my effort toward flattering him, toward making him like me and feel good. But not with Lennox. He likes the bickering, the fighting. It's the only way he and I connect.

"You don't want me to fuck you, Rialta."

My breath catches when he calls me by my name. I could get used to the seductive way he says it.

No, I couldn't. I hate it.

He cocks his head as if he can hear my internal conflict. "I can see through you, Rialta. You think you still care about Kit. You still wish you could take him back, but if you fuck me, you know he'd never take you back. The decision would be made for you. And it would come with the added bonus of punishing him and getting back some of your pride. But I'm not going to help you do it."

He starts to walk past me, but I move in front of him, blocking the door. "Why? You wanted to fuck me. You even bet me that I would beg you to fuck you. You would win that bet if we did. Kit would be out of our lives forever. You would be protecting the friends you say you care about." I hesitate. "And you can hate fuck me like I know you want to."

"Beg."

"What?"

"The key word of our bet was that you would *beg* me. This pathetic pleading is far from begging."

"Please, Lennox, will you fuck me? Pretty please?" my voice is dripping with sarcasm. I won't beg.

Lennox takes a step toward me. I don't move. Our chests are barely touching. Suddenly his hand tangles in my hair, his roughness sending shockwaves through my body. He already owns me. It's only a matter of time until I'm on my knees begging for everything he can give me.

Everything stops as he tugs on my hair, tilting my head so our lips are almost brushing. "I don't fuck women that don't want me. As you learned the other night, when I protected your precious virginity."

"I'm not a virgin."

He scoffs. "Maybe not technically, but I heard the way that boy fucked you. That, my dear Rialta, is not fucking. When I fuck you, you will realize that you've never been fucked before."

"Then do it and prove me wrong."

He releases me. "No."

He slides me to one side and walks past me, leaving me breathless in the doorway, still topless, still needing something, and no closer to actually getting it.

Beg, he said.

I can't beg.

I can barely force myself to continue on with this plan. It hurts me enough to ask, let alone beg. But I need him to fuck me. It's the only way.

I turn and find Lennox stripping out of his jeans, wincing as he does.

"Sit on the bed," I say, putting the thoughts of sex out of my head as I realize he's injured.

He does as I say, probably because he's in too much pain.

He's lowered his jeans to mid-thigh, but not any further.

"Is it a bullet?" I ask.

He shakes his head. "No, stab wound."

My eyes widen.

"Don't be shocked, Rialta. I'm fine. But the dried blood has the jeans stuck to my thigh. I need to get them off and clean it before infection sets in. Otherwise, you'll never get to find out what it's like to be fucked by me."

I roll my eyes. "I'm beginning to think I'm a fool for wanting to have sex with you at all."

"Well, that's definitely true. Once I fuck you, you'll never want another man ever again."

I swallow hard, slightly afraid that he might be right.

"What do you want me to do?" I ask.

"Pull the jeans off."

"Won't that hurt?"

"Yes, but it has to be done. If you won't—"

I yank the jeans off like ripping a bandaid. I expect a howl of pain or growling, but he doesn't make a sound. When I look into his eyes, there's a spark of mischief—he's pleased by my actions.

I stare down at the deep wound surrounded by black tattoos around his thighs and creeping up beneath his boxers like an invitation to see what lies beneath. I ignore how hot I feel and instead examine the wound. It looks like it needs stitches or a doctor, but I know he won't get either. Whatever care I provide is all he's going to get. As much as I hate the man, I don't want him to die. That would only further complicate my life.

"Don't move," I say before running downstairs. I grab what Lennox didn't use of the first aid kit on Hayes and run back upstairs.

Lennox is still sitting on the edge of the bed in just his black boxer briefs. Tattoos cover his body from head to toe.

His reddish brown hair is dripping water down his bare shoulders.

I bite my lip as I look at him and feel an ache deep in my belly. It's something more than just a solution to my problem—a true wanting. It rattles me and almost knocks me on my ass to feel attracted to this man at a time like this.

"Are you just going to stare at me while I bleed out?"

I roll my eyes and stomp over, kneeling between his legs so I can get a good look at the wound on his inner thigh. "You're not going to bleed out. Stop being so dramatic."

I take some antiseptic and clean the wound before looking at the supplies. All that's left is a bandage barely large enough to cover the gash, but I'm not sure it's going to be enough.

"It will do," Lennox says, reading my mind.

I nod and place the bandage over the wound before wrapping gauze around his thigh several times to secure it. I'm examining my work, happy that at least it has a chance of healing and not getting infected, when my eyes lock on a different region.

I stare at the hardness beneath his boxer briefs as I kneel in front of him. I don't move. He can tell I'm staring, that I see how turned on he is. He wants me; there is no denying that.

"A half-naked woman is kneeling in front of my cock. Of course, I'm hard," he says.

"Liar."

My eyes meet his, and I see the gleam of truth twinkling in his eyes. "You want me, not just any woman."

"You won't be finding out, Rialta. Not until you beg for it."

I won't beg.

But I don't think he'll be able to resist. I make my move.

I grab his boxer briefs and slide them quickly down his

body just as I did his jeans, until he's naked in front of me. I'm still kneeling, and my eyes glaze over, staring at his glorious cock, just begging for me to suck it.

I've never wanted to suck a cock more. I'm entranced by the way it grows larger under my gaze.

Kit flicks into my head, and I realize how easy it would be to pretend that Lennox's cock is Kit's.

But I don't want to.

The words hit me like a bullet to the heart. I wasn't expecting to feel this way.

Lennox stands and walks around me, leaving me empty. "I'm not fucking you and letting you pretend I'm him. And I'm not fucking you so that you can forget him, either. You're not going to use me."

I hear hurt, anger, and pain in his voice. I've disappointed him when all he's ever done is try to protect me.

I'm still kneeling as I turn to face him. "If I'm thinking about him, it's only because I realize how truly over my relationship with him really is."

Lennox narrows his eyes at me as I speak—cautiously suspicious of every word I'm saying.

"Kit didn't cheat on me. I broke up with him. I ended things. It's over." I pause, letting my words sink in. My eyes meet his, and I pour every emotion I have into my gaze. I let him see how vulnerable I am, how truthful I'm being.

"I want you, Lennox—not to heal my broken heart, but just because I want you. I've wanted you for a long time, but I didn't want to admit it to myself, let alone you. I've wanted you since you saved me on our wedding night."

Lennox doesn't speak, so I have no idea if he believes me. No idea if my words mean anything. So finally, I say the words that he wants to hear.

"Please, Lennox. Please fuck me. Please let me suck your cock. Please, I'm begging you."

CHAPTER 25

Lennox

I STARE at Rialta kneeling on the floor in front of me. She's half-naked, her breasts begging me to touch them, along with the words that fell from her pretty lips. She's a complete fucking disaster. Her jeans are covered in Hayes's blood, her hair is draped messily over one shoulder, and her makeup is smeared. And yet my cock thinks she's the most beautiful, sexy woman in the whole world—like she's fucking Aphrodite or something.

Gone is any thought of the attack we just endured or what the implications of it are. Gone is my worry for Hayes or that we could be attacked again. All I can focus on is her.

Jesus, what am I doing?

I know what I'm about to do, and it's probably one of the most foolish things I've ever done.

Rialta's not telling me the whole truth. I'm not sure I believe that she's not thinking about him or that she doesn't want to fuck me just to piss him off or erase memories of him from her mind. But I am convinced that this is what she truly wants. If I do fuck her, she's not going to have regrets two minutes later. Regardless of whatever happened in the past, this is what she wants going forward.

I can't fault her for lying. I'm not telling the entire truth either, so it's only fair that she's doing the same.

God, do I fucking want her.

But fucking her would make my life easier and harder at the same time. It's what I've wanted, what I've been working toward this whole time. I needed to get rid of that asshole to have a chance for her to fall in love with me. I have the better part of a year left to make it happen. And this is that first step.

Please—her words make my cock twitch, and it takes everything inside me not to run over to her, fist her hair, and part her lips with my cock down her throat.

Now to test how sincere her begging really is.

I crook my finger at her, telling her to come here with a single action. I doubt she will obey; she likes to fight me at every turn.

But Rialta does exactly what I want. She crawls toward me, not even bothering to stand. Her eyes are fixated on me, and my cock grows harder with every inch she moves toward me. And then she's kneeling in front of me, her large innocent-looking eyes staring up at me as my cock grows towards her lips.

Her eyes flick down toward it, and she licks her lips in anticipation.

I twist my hand into her hair, finally allowing myself what I've wanted this whole time.

"Suck," I command.

I expect a snarky comment. I expect her to want to discuss this more. I don't expect her to open her mouth wide and wrap her lips around the tip without argument.

Her lips touch me, and I shatter.

My world changes with the brush of her lips against my

cock. I haven't had a woman touch me in an intimate way in forever. And I wasn't prepared to have anyone touch me now.

Our eyes lock as she slowly and meticulously slides her lips from the tip down my shaft, taking more and more of me in her mouth. I'm not sure how far she's willing to go, but it's fucking incredible to watch her suck me. Every other thought and worry float out of my head as she sucks me.

I don't react outwardly, though. I don't let her know how her single touch affects me so. And she doesn't show any signs of wanting to stop, nor how good my cock tastes as she swirls her tongue around the tip. We're in a standoff.

"Show me how much you want my cock."

The second I say the words, it's like I've given her permission to enjoy what she's doing.

She closes her eyes and moans as she takes me deeper and deeper in her throat.

God, she's perfect.

Her whimpering and soft moans get louder and louder as she gets bolder with her strokes.

"Look at me," I say, afraid her eyes will be glazed over with thoughts of *him*.

When she looks at me, her eyes darken, and there's a small twinkle in her eye as her teeth scrape my skin gently before sucking harder, making me gasp and almost lose my load.

"Wicked thing," I sputter when I regain my composure.

She grins around my cock, entirely present.

I pull her head back off my cock, even though it pains me to do it. All I want is to have her continue to beg and suck me on her knees in front of me. I need to see what's changed. I need to see if she is truly ready for this. If this is what she wants.

Seeing her on her knees—this is definitely what I want.

And more than just because it's what will help me cement my deal with Vincent and stay alive. I want Rialta.

But only if she wants me in return. I don't want to fuck her to erase Kit. And I don't want her to fuck me for any other reason than she wants to fuck me.

She's close to coming to that realization, even if her motives for wanting to fuck me started off differently.

"Lay down on the bed," I command.

Her eyes widen, and her teeth scrape her bottom lip, but she obeys. She takes her time, lying down on the bed. Her chest rises and falls quickly, drawing my attention to her curvaceous breasts that have been begging for me to touch them and lick their peaks. It's taking all my self-control to not touch her until I'm sure she couldn't take another breath if I didn't fuck her.

I walk to my closet, feeling her eyes on my naked body as I walk. It's a feeling I could get used to.

I take my time in the closet, knowing I'm driving her wild with anxiety and anticipation. When I step back out, I don't let her see what's in my hands straight away.

"Trust me," I demand, not asking.

"I trust you, Lennox, more than I trust myself."

Her words pull at my heart. She should trust herself. Her instincts are better than she realizes, and it's not trusting herself that has led her to some bad decisions. But that's a conversation for a different time.

"Put your hands above your head."

Her eyes stay on me as she slowly raises her hands above her head, her back arching as she does, pushing her breasts toward me, inviting me to touch her.

Not yet—patience.

I walk to the head of the bed, where her arms are stretched. I continue to stare at her—to keep her focus on me. To keep her present with me. To notice any doubt or flickering back to him.

Her eyes stay locked on me with lust and desire.

Let's see how much she really trusts me.

I reveal the tie I found in my closet and begin to tie her wrists together.

She freezes, and I think maybe I made the wrong decision. I don't know all of her past. I don't know if any man has ever tied her up or if she even likes this sort of thing. But my instincts told me she needs me to control her. She liked the other night when I spanked her, when I was rough with her. She liked it but didn't want to admit it out loud.

But I could be wrong.

And if I'm wrong, I could ruin everything.

I study her closely as I continue to tie her wrists. I can see her pulse jumping wildly in her throat. Her eyes dilate with a twinkle of fear and doubt.

She's not gone. She's not with Kit. She's not lost to some dark past.

I lean down and kiss that spot on her neck where I can see her pulse racing. "Trust me. I won't hurt you. I won't do anything you won't enjoy. All you have to do is tell me to stop, and I will—at any time." I kiss her again and watch her shiver, accepting my words.

"Please," she whimpers. It's not a plea to stop. It's a plea to keep my promise, and it's the sweetest sound I've ever heard.

"I've got you." I kiss her earlobe and tie her to my metal headboard. Then I step back, admiring her.

"So fucking hot."

She blushes, shaking her head. "I'm a mess."

I shake my head hungrily. "No, if you could see you how I see you, you'd realize how fucking incredible you are."

She looks into my eyes and sees how badly I want her.

I inch up the bed, my hands gliding up her jeans until I reach the button. She licks her lips, waiting impatiently for me to remove her jeans.

But I milk my every move.

I undo the button.

Then the zipper.

Then I kiss her belly button sweetly, gently, torturously.

"You're going to kill me," she says, gasping at every little kiss.

"I'm going to kill us both." I hook my hands into her jeans, and she lifts her hips as I pull until she's left in nothing but a black thong.

"Please," she purrs again.

I grin.

Tying her up was my best fucking decision. She can't do anything but writhe and wiggle and *beg*. I didn't realize how hard her begging would make me.

I hook my fingers under the straps of her thong and yank them down next, wanting to see how fucking beautiful I know she is, wanting to see all of her. I ball up her panties, feeling the dampness there. She's wet, but not wet enough for what I have planned next.

Then, my eyes return to her.

"Fuck," I groan at the sight of her completely naked, completely mine.

Mine.

But she's not mine, not really. She wants sex, but that doesn't change her feelings for me. It doesn't make her mine. After I fuck her, she'll go right back to hating and arguing with me.

That word has already taken root, though. *Mine*—I want her to be mine, not just the woman I fuck tonight. But I have no idea how to do that.

For now, I'll enjoy her.

I crawl up the bed between her legs, my eyes dragging over every inch of her body. Her smooth, warm skin makes me want to run my tongue all over to taste every bit of her. I spread her legs as I lower my face over her belly button, kissing her so soft and tenderly. Really, I want to spank her, dig my teeth into her flesh, and mark her over and over until it's clear to everyone that she's mine.

Mine, mine, mine.

Jesus, what's wrong with me?

I kiss lower.

She shifts on the bed, waiting in anticipation of the pleasure I can give her. But I'm not going to take it further until she's begging. Until I'm sure this is what she wants with everything in her body.

I kiss her hip bone.

She shivers, arching her back so she can see what I'm doing.

I kiss just inside her hip, moving lower but so slowly that it could take me years to reach her swollen bud at the pace I'm going.

I kiss again, this time letting my teeth scrape against her skin.

"Lennox, please."

"Please, what?" I ask, grinning manically as I kiss the inside of her thigh.

"I need you to fuck me."

"Hmm, do you now?"

"Yes, please, I'm losing my mind. I need you." Her words are panicked and needy and exactly what I want to hear.

I reward her by kissing her clit and sucking hard. The sound she makes at my touch is burned into my memory for the rest of time.

I force myself to stop, to give her a chance to change her

mind. The second I stop, she bucks her hips upward, begging me with her body to keep going.

Our eyes lock, and I see the desperation and need there. I'm so hungry for more of her—for all of her. And when I look at her, I see my desire reflected in her eyes.

"Please." It's a whisper, so sincere.

I lick my tongue up her slit, enjoying every drop of her sweet wetness as it fills my tongue.

And then I let myself loose.

I lick her hungrily, devouring all of her. My fingers dig into her ass, lifting her up so I can take more of her in.

I could stay here forever, feasting on her, listening to the moans and whimpers leaving her body. They start off soft and controlled but quickly grow faster, louder, and wild.

I want to bring her all the pleasure in the world and punish her simultaneously. I slip two fingers inside her, and the most delicious gasp curls up her throat. I'm both pleased and want to punish her for feeling anything good.

As I thrust my fingers inside her, feeling her tightness grip me and her legs tighten around my face, I know I'm going to let her come. I need it as much as she does.

I lick faster over her swollen clit, sliding my fingers in and out of her rhythmically as she rocks her hips into me.

"Come, Rialta."

She does. Her legs tremble around my head, her walls tighten around my fingers, and the sweet cry from her lips almost makes me come.

I step back, examining her. Her face is flushed—still shocked by the orgasm I just gave her. Her eyes are closed, and her body is still trembling.

"Rialta, what do you want?" I ask, my voice dark and menacing.

I want to fuck her. I need to be inside her. I need to punish her with my dick and then, later, spank her, tie her up, and rip her apart. She sparks such dark desires in me, desires that scare the shit out of me. They would scare the shit out of her, too, if she knew what was going on in my head.

I've never been like this. I've fucked plenty of women, but never wanted to tie them up, never wanted to dominate them, never wanted...

I shake my head. It's probably just because of our hate-hate relationship that makes me want to do devilish things to her.

She blinks her eyes open as if in a daze, but then her eyes find mine. I know she sees the darkness there. She sees how I'm panting with my hands fisting by my side as I wait impatiently for her to answer. She sees the edge of my barely controlled rage and desire for her. She sees me—the monster beneath the exterior.

She's going to tell me to stop, to untie her, that she's had enough. I know it. I don't know how I'm going to get my control back if she does. I may have to leave her tied and go get my pent-up emotions out somewhere else while I send Gage to untie her. I'm not sure I trust myself enough to let her go without making her mine.

Her eyes grow heavy, and her voice raspy. "Fuck me, Lennox. Fuck me with everything you have, and in all the ways you want. I'm yours."

CHAPTER 26

Rialta

I CAN BARELY CONTROL my breathing. I can't control anything. And I'm not sure I want to. Whatever darkness flickered into Lennox's eyes—that's what I want.

He growls deeply—it's meant to scare me, but it doesn't. He doesn't scare me.

I want him. *All of him.*

I want his tenderness and his roughness.

I want the man who just gave me the sweetest release and then looked at me like he wants to fuck me so hard I should fear him. And I want whatever fantasy he just thought up.

I've never had sex in any way but traditional—missionary, doggy style, girl on top. That about covers my sexual history.

Having my arms tied above my head is spicier than anything I've ever tried before. Kit never tied me up. And he was the only man I've ever been with.

I thought I wanted to be in control. That I wouldn't ever want a man to dominate me—especially in the bedroom. But watching Lennox stand over me as I'm tied, completely at his mercy, I've never been so hot, never wanted sex more.

I push down what that means. I loved Kit. No, I *love* Kit. But I *desire* Lennox.

And Kit and I are over. It was confirmed the second Lennox gave me the best damn orgasm of my life.

I'll admit it to myself but not to Lennox. *He doesn't need to know that.*

I don't think Lennox will unleash himself when he fucks me, but I want him to. I want what his eyes promise. But I'm also not sure he can hold back.

He walks to the nightstand, pulling out a box of condoms.

I raise an eyebrow. "You won the bet. This is me begging for your cock. You get to have an heir."

Lennox stills, holding a condom pulled from the box. He considers my offer but continues with the condom as he walks toward the bed. I'm still tied, my legs spread lazily apart. I don't bother to try and cover myself. I like his eyes on my body, and I don't feel any shame.

Lennox rips the condom wrapper open and rolls it onto his hard cock. "I may have won the bet, but we'll discuss the details of when I claim my prize later. This isn't about the bet."

This isn't about the bet.

His words affirm what I already suspected. Then he's standing at the foot of the bed with nothing left to do but fuck me.

I wait.

But he doesn't move.

I stare at him—his sculpted body covered in tattoos. His sheathed cock straining, ready to fuck me. But yet, he waits as if he still doesn't believe this is going to happen, even now. As if he's waiting for me to beg him to stop.

Our eyes meet, and I make it clear in them that there is nothing that's going to make me change my mind about this. I'm sure.

"Fuck me," I whisper across my lips. I'm soaked, I'm flushed, and I'm more than ready for him.

"You have no idea what you're asking for, dear *wife*."

It's the first time he's called me that in private. But it makes it clear his intentions—when he fucks me, he's claiming me. This is as much about having sex as it is about making me his.

I don't know what's going to happen after we fuck, just that I won't have any regrets.

He grins wickedly as he climbs over my body. His hand runs up the curve of my hip, dragging his nails into my flesh as he moves up until his hand is around my neck.

"Beg for me, wife. Beg me to fuck you. To show you what it's like to be fucked, controlled, made mine." His hand tightens around my neck, making it hard for me to breathe. His eyes are wild with want and crazed desire.

He's trying to scare me, but still, I'm unafraid. I let my eyes grow heavy with my own desire. I need him to fuck me.

Then his mouth lowers over mine in a rough kiss. Our lips meld together as his slick tongue slips into my mouth, demanding I open for him.

I spread my legs and arch my hips, begging for him to enter me. I realize just how ready I am for him.

He doesn't ask permission—not again.

But his hand reaches between my legs, testing my wetness once more before his cock pushes at my entrance.

I hold my breath, knowing this is the moment I can't take back. Everything before this moment could be forgiven, but not this.

My arms are still stretched above my head, tied to the

bed, but I've never felt in control of this decision more than now.

He hesitates. He's a controlling alpha, but in this moment, he's relenting the control he wants to me. I don't know what in his past has made him so hesitant, but I respect him for it.

He thrusts.

I roll my hips.

And he slams into me.

I gasp as he fills me. I've never felt so full. My head falls back, and he stops.

"Last chance, wife. Neither of us is going to be able to stop after this," Lennox says.

His words give me a hint at what his dark desires are and what his past is. *Did he fuck a woman who told him to stop, and he couldn't?*

But I know there is no way I'm going to want to stop this. He's not going to hurt me. At least he won't hurt me more than the physical act of sex would.

When I kiss him hard, sucking his bottom lip into my mouth, he unleashes himself.

He thrusts into me so hard that my eyes water. His hand tightens around my throat as he sinks his teeth just above my clavicle.

I whimper at the sensations pulsing through my body. His thrusts are more intense than anything I've ever felt. My head is spinning with how I'm going to survive the intensity of this.

His hand runs down the curves of my body until he's grabbed my ass. He spanks me hard, and I cry out, but it only makes me wetter.

His cock is full and thick inside me, pounding into me deep in my core.

I can't move. I can't think. I can barely breathe as he fucks me.

I'm thankful he tied my arms. I'm not sure how to respond to him, and I'd feel like I couldn't keep up if he let me have any physical control.

"Come, wife."

I don't think I'm close. I'm all over the place, barely staying present. But his fingers pinch my clit, and I explode all over his dick.

Convulsing, my head is spinning.

"You have no idea all the things I plan on doing to you, wife. Being tied like this is nothing compared to what I really want." He nips at my earlobe. "I want you covered in ropes so you can't move a single muscle without my say so. I want to paint your ass red with my hand. I want you on your knees, submitting to my every command."

I swallow hard, not ready to admit out loud how hot and turned I am by the thought of him doing any of those things. I'm not ready to admit that I want this more than once. That will be a decision for tomorrow after my head clears.

He smirks, seeing my need on my face.

I blush.

"Don't you dare blush for having fantasies. Especially when they're fantasies I'm very willing to fulfill."

"They're not my fantasies—they're yours," I whisper back. But even as I say it, I know that's not true. My own mind is whizzing with the different positions we could get into. Visions flood my mind of the ways he could dominate my body and make me feel things I've never felt with any other man before.

He shakes his head, still grinning like a fool.

His hand palms my breast, and I'm lost to his touch again. He takes my nipple between his thumb and finger, pinching the tip until I'm on the edge again, all the while continuing to pound into me.

I don't know how he has such self-control or how he lasts so long without unloading inside me.

And just as I think it, I see the flicker of craze in his eyes, and I know he can't hold on much longer. He needs to let go. He needs to come.

"Not yet. Not until you've come again." He pauses. "And again."

There is no way I'm going to come twice more. But with another flick of my nipple, I'm coming at his mercy. My mind is whirling. I can't think straight. My breath is coming so fast that it's overwhelming and intense and...fuck, I want to come again.

He stills inside me, just watching me in awe. It gives me a second to catch my breath before he ruins me again.

He kisses my neck.

I shiver.

"One more," he breathes.

"I can't," I whimper.

He smiles smugly. "You have no idea what you're capable of yet."

I don't know what he means by that, but then he's thrusting inside me, and I can't think about anything other than him.

I want more. So much more.

In my mind, this was only going to happen tonight. And then maybe a couple of times a month to try and get pregnant if that's what Lennox wanted. But not more. This wasn't supposed to become anything real.

Lennox's eyes match mine—there's fear in his, same as mine. Fear and realization that this is more than either of us bargained for.

His body rubs against mine until I feel him everywhere, from my head to my toes and deep in my core.

This time he doesn't have to coax an orgasm from me—I give it willingly, knowing I can't stop it, just like I can't stop whatever is happening between us.

I contract hard around his cock, and he loses control. His orgasm spills through his body as he moans into my bare shoulder, his teeth sink into my flesh, making me cry out in delicious ecstasy.

We each stay still after our orgasms have subsided. Our breathing regulates, matching each other. We are more in sync than we've ever been before, but it won't last. Things have changed completely between us, but I suspect we'll go back to bickering as soon as we get our clothes on.

Lennox stands up and walks to the bathroom, leaving me tied naked to his bed.

I don't mind. It gives me time to just be without thinking about what I should do or say or feel. I just bask in the glow of my multiple orgasms.

A soft smile rests on my lips as Lennox returns from the bathroom. He walks to the closet and then comes back out in loose athletic shorts.

He stares at me on the bed, and I think he's finally going to say something.

He walks over to the top of the bed, unties the knot on the tie, and then he jogs down the stairs without a word to me.

I take a deep breath.

It's done.

I pull the covers over me, not even bothering to clean up. I'll deal with the aftermath tomorrow. Right now, I just want to enjoy the feeling of peace flowing throughout my body and knowing that, for once, I made the right decision.

I DON'T TRUST myself with Rialta. I don't trust any of my emotions. So many vile and defiling things I want to do to her pop into my head as I watch her lay naked, tied to my bed. I haven't had my fill of her. Not nearly enough.

Neither of us is satiated. Even though I gave her multiple orgasms, I know she hasn't had enough. She's not mine yet. She doesn't love me yet.

But she will.

She'll love me for the sex, if nothing else, because that boyfriend of hers never made her feel like I did in a single hour together. I'm barely learning her body, barely figuring out what she likes and dislikes. When I do, she'll never want to leave my bed.

That is, if I can keep my sinful desires to myself. She liked being tied up, the occasional slap and sinking of my teeth, but she won't like the fantasies consuming my mind. She won't like to be truly dominated and controlled and spanked until her skin is red.

So I'll keep those thoughts to myself.

I head into Hayes and Gage's apartment, focusing my

attention on Hayes until I can think clearly again. I find them both in Hayes's bedroom. Hayes is in bed. Gage is sitting in a chair watching him.

"How is he?" I ask Gage.

"He's alive and doing just fine. You should ask him how he's doing instead of talking over him and treating him like he's a child," Hayes answers.

I roll my eyes, and Gage just shrugs. *Typical Hayes.*

"Glad you're back in fighting spirit," I say.

"I'm fine—I don't know what you all are fussing about. It's just a scratch. I don't feel a thing," Hayes says.

"That's because you're filled with pain meds and high as fuck," Gage says.

Hayes frowns at him.

"It's true. That wound was bad. You almost died. If it wasn't for Rialta having the right blood type, you probably would have died," I say.

"Well, I'm alive now, so you two can stop your fussing over me and figure out what we are going to do about the Retribution Kings."

I take a deep breath. "We all know what we have to do." We thought we'd have more time, but then Corsi moved up our timetable when he made me kill one of the Retribution Kings.

Even though the Kings are operating without a leader currently, they attacked us. They couldn't let my murder go without a response. And the attack isn't enough to get the revenge they seek. They won't stop until they kill me or someone I love—that's the only appropriate retribution.

Gage shakes his head. "No."

"I agree with Gage, no," says Hayes.

I fold my arms and glare at both of them. "It's the plan we agreed to. If this is to work, then we have to follow the plan. It's time."

"No," they both say in unison.

I shake my head. "Then when? We all die? Next time, Hayes could really die, or you could, Gage. Next time they won't let you live!" My voice is serious and harsh, but I need them to see things my way. I'm not their boss, not really, but it's moments like this that I wish I was. Most of the time, it isn't an issue. Most of the time, they follow my orders without a second thought. But decisions like this I can't make alone. They won't let me.

"How's it going with Rialta?" Hayes asks suddenly, smirking at me and changing the subject completely.

"She's fine," I answer, not giving anything away.

He laughs. "You reek of sex, Lennox. Seems like it's going better than fine."

"I need to go check on her. Glad you're still alive, asshole."

Hayes continues to laugh as I walk back to my apartment, feeling more unsettled than ever. I know what needs to be done about the Retribution Kings. We can't keep having them attack like this. We won't survive if we don't have the full support of Corsi and his men to keep the Retribution Kings at bay, which we won't have until I prove to Vincent I love his daughter and get her pregnant or destroy their enemy. Either of which will be a long time from now, and Hayes or Gage could end up dead in the meantime.

I run my hand through my hair, feeling my anxiety creeping up again. I'll have to find a way to protect them, just like I have to protect Rialta. And I need to find some men in the Corsi organization that I trust. I can't rely on Beckett or Ri anymore now that they're pregnant. I feel like I'm on my own protecting everyone else, and I don't know how much longer I can hold on.

I find Rialta asleep in my bed. She hasn't bothered to get

dressed, and the covers have inched down her body, bunched at her waist.

She's beautiful—there's no denying that. If I had a heart left to give, I'd give it to her.

But I don't.

I can't fall in love.

All I can offer her is as much protection as I can muster.

I watch her sleep. I don't know how much time passes, but I just sit on the end of the bed and watch her. I could watch her all day and night. Call me a creepy stalker.

Her eyes eventually flutter open, staring right at me with a warm smile like she knew I was watching her sleep this entire time. She doesn't move to cover her naked body. She's not the least bit ashamed, but I have to ask...

"Any regrets?"

"No," she responds immediately. She sits up in bed, and I can't help but stare at her voluptuous breasts. I want to feel them in my hands again.

"What about you? You couldn't run out of here fast enough."

I snicker. "No, I don't regret fucking you, even if you didn't deserve to be fucked like that. You especially didn't earn those three orgasms."

Her eyes sneer. "I thought my begging earned me exactly what I got. Don't count on me begging again." She gets out of the bed and walks to the closet, my eyes following her every move.

When she comes back out, she's wearing one of my white T-shirts and nothing else. She's going to drive me mad all day, teasing and trying to get me to fuck her again without her having to beg. Which means she wants to fuck again even if her mouth is saying something different.

She tries to move past me, but I stand from the bed and

block her. "It seems you still want to play games, even though I won our first one."

"You won the bet, but it seems you aren't ready to collect." Her eyes flick to the condom wrapper.

My eyes darken. "Oh, I plan on collecting, wife. But I want to make sure you're clean before I impregnate you. Who knows what that boy of yours gave you."

She frowns. "And who knows what your latest conquest gave you."

She's fishing, wanting to know when the last time I had sex before her was. But that would reveal too much about me, so it's not something she gets to know.

There's a knock on the door, and my heart jumps. I pull out my phone, looking to see if Gage sent an alarm text, but there's nothing.

I look at Rialta, and I notice she looks weary but not scared at all. She knows who is knocking because she called him here.

I march downstairs with Rialta fast on my heels as I open the door and find Kit standing there. I realize that I won the bet, but Rialta won the game. She used me to break up with Kit.

I glance back at her standing in my shirt. She's wearing it not because she wants to tease me but because she wants to make it completely clear to Kit what transpired here.

"I'm sorry," she says, most likely to Kit. But it feels like a part of her is apologizing to me too.

"I don't believe you," Kit says, his eyes widen as he glances past me shirtless to her wearing only my shirt. He pushes under my arm, gripping the doorframe, and goes to her.

She backs away, determined not to let him touch her. She doesn't have to worry; he stops immediately when he gets a whiff of her.

Kit knows exactly what happened. He can smell me on her.

He backs away. "You're a fucking slut. I can't believe I ever loved you. I can't believe—"

I grab him by the neck and drag him out of my apartment. "If you ever talk to my wife like that again, it will be with your last breath." I don't kill him now because he's just a heartbroken, silly fool. And Rialta still cares about him as much as she won't admit it. "Now leave."

I don't have to tell him twice. He practically runs down the hall away from me.

I shut the door and face Rialta, who doesn't look the least bit ashamed by what she did. She folds her arms across her chest and holds her head high.

"I'm impressed. But I knew you were lying when you said you had already broken up with him. I just didn't know why. It turns out you're trying to keep him safe by letting him go."

I step closer into her personal space. She doesn't back up or surrender. I tuck a long thick strip of her flowing brown hair behind her ear.

"But what you don't know is saying you wanted me was more truthful than anything else you've ever said to me. You can think you love him all you want, but the truth is you want me. You crave me. And soon, you'll be addicted to me. Love is a silly emotion that always ends up leaving you broken. But want, desire, need—those emotions are something you can have power over. They won't hurt you like he just did."

"He didn't hurt me."

"Then why did you wince when he called you a slut? Why did your heart break a little when he ran out that door less than a minute after he walked in and didn't fight for you?"

She doesn't answer.

"Exactly—it hurt you. I won't hurt you, my dear wife. At least not emotionally. Now physically, sexually—I plan on tormenting you, pushing you to the edge of tolerance to see where your limits are. I'll make you stronger when I'm done with you. I won't leave you broken and hurt."

I take her hand and kiss her wrist, where there is still a little redness from where I tied her up. "I'll just leave my mark. And now that you're mine completely, I plan on letting everyone know by marking every inch of your body as mine."

"I'm not yours. I surrendered. I just lost a bet because I loved a man more than I cared about winning the bet."

I give her a sly smile. "That's what you say, but deep down, you know the truth. When I fucked you, it changed things. Not just between us. It changed you. It changed what you want. And soon you'll realize that."

CHAPTER 28

Rialta

"HOW ARE YOU DOING?" I ask Hayes as I walk over to the chair next to his bed.

Hayes grins at me with a bright, charming smile. Nothing ever gets him down, even being unable to get out of bed and in incredible pain from that bullet wound.

Gage said it will take him at least a week before he should be getting out of bed, longer than that to get back into the shape he was before. I can already tell it's driving him crazy to be stuck in bed and not be able to help and plan.

"Fantastic, thanks to you."

I shake my head as I sink into my seat. "You saved me first; it was only fair I repaid the favor."

His grin widens. "And that kiss was something, sweetheart. Care to try again? Now that I'm awake, I can show how well I can really kiss."

His eyes twinkle mischievously, and I know he's just teasing me. He's trying to figure out what's going on between Lennox and me.

Honestly, I have no idea what's going on with Lennox

and me. After Lennox found out the truth about my plan with Kit, he hasn't spoken to me since. And I haven't pushed him.

I got what I wanted—I think.

I blush, thinking about the fantasies that have constantly been flowing through my head since Lennox fucked me. I wanted to protect Kit. I wanted to protect them all, and I knew the only way to do it was to let Kit go.

I still love Kit; I'll probably always love him. But I have to accept my future is with Lennox, whether I like it or not. And I might as well enjoy the sex if I can't enjoy the rest of it.

"Stop trying to stir up trouble, Hayes," I say.

"Trouble? I'd never stir up trouble. But I heard you and your boyfriend broke it off, so I thought there might be an opening?" He wiggles his eyebrows at me.

I roll my eyes. "I'm not looking for a boyfriend."

"Because you already have a husband that can fulfill your needs?"

"I think Gage has been giving you too many pain meds if you think I'm going to answer that question."

There's a soft knock on the door, and then River pokes her head in. Her eyes drop when she sees Hayes laid up in the bed.

"Cheer up, Ri. I'll be good as new in a week or so," Hayes says gleefully, hiding any ounce of pain. Even with the pain meds, I'm sure he's in pain. He has to be.

River walks over to the other side of the bed and squeezes his hand in hers, relieved to see him alive and well. Beckett enters the room next and makes some joke I don't hear because all I can focus on is River's growing bump.

She's going to be a mother in a matter of months. And if Lennox gets his way, I'll be pregnant soon after.

I swallow hard at the lump in my throat.

So many lives are hindering on me. On Lennox. On Vincent Corsi and his men keeping us safe.

I have an enemy that wants me and the Corsi line dead. And now the Retribution Kings have been added to the list of enemies.

And River's baby doesn't deserve to be in danger. None of them do because of me.

There's another knock on the door, and Lennox steps in. "We should get going soon."

I nod, getting up. But then I hear River and Beckett saying their goodbyes to Hayes as well, even though they just got here.

"What are you doing?" I ask River.

"We're going with you. We need to keep you safe, and it's clear now that the Retribution Kings are after you that you need all the protection you can get until we convince Vincent to offer more," River says.

"No, you're not coming. It's not safe," I say.

River frowns. "I can take care of myself better than anyone here. And if you die, and I wasn't there to protect you, I couldn't live with myself."

"You're pregnant. I couldn't live with myself if anything happened to you or the baby."

"Nothing's going to happen. I won't let it," River says.

I look to Beckett, knowing if I can't convince River, then I can convince him. But he's tight-lipped, and when he meets my gaze, it's clear that he's letting River make the decision. He can't change anything.

It means we have to convince my father to give us more men for security. We have to convince him and the men to follow Lennox as my father's successor. We have to find men in Vincent's ranks that we can actually trust.

Hayes being down for a week and longer before he can actually protect or fight. Gage spending his time tending to

Hayes. River pregnant. Beckett needing to protect River. And more enemies coming after us—this plan has to work, or we'll all end up dead.

Gage enters the room. "I'm sorry I can't come with you."

"Of course, you're going with them," Hayes says.

Everyone turns and looks at him.

"I'm not leaving you without any protection," Gage says.

"Then I'm going too," Hayes says defiantly. It's the most I've ever seen him fight back.

Gage, Beckett, and Lennox's eyes all meet, and they have a silent conversation. *Should they force him to stay or come with?*

I look at River, who is looking at me like it's my decision.

All I can think is it has to be Hayes's choice. Just like River's decision is her own. And my life is my own choice.

There is no place that's safe anymore. It doesn't matter if he's here or with us. And based on everyone's actions, it feels like we'd all rather stick together as much as possible.

"Come if you want, but be honest with how you're feeling. If you're in pain, tell Gage. Promise not to push yourself?" I look Hayes in the eyes, telling him I'll wring his neck if he hurts himself on my behalf.

He nods solemnly.

I feel the unease of everyone else around me. No one wants Hayes to push himself or get hurt, but that could happen just as easily if he stays behind.

———

We all crowd in Vincent's office. There are only three chairs. Hayes, River, and I are the ones sitting, while the others stand in the chairs behind us.

It was a wasted trip. Vincent isn't going to change his mind, even to protect his own daughters.

"We need more security. I can't keep her safe from the entire fucking world if I don't have the resources and team to do it. Especially when you keep creating enemies," Lennox says, glaring at Vincent.

Vincent sits behind his desk, showing no emotion as Lennox pleads his case.

"No," is all he says.

Lennox runs his hand through his hair and paces behind me. I can feel his frustration pouring off him in waves. He wants to climb over Vincent's desk and strangle him.

"We need help. Lennox is doing everything he can to keep me safe. Everyone here is. But it won't be enough. Hayes almost died last night. It could have just as easily been me," I say, looking my father in his eyes. Hoping if I beg him, he'll change his mind. I'll still end up dead sooner than later, but I want to take as few people as possible with me when my time comes.

Vincent looks from me to every person in the room, taking his time perusing each and every one of us as if he thinks one of us has the answer.

"I trust everyone in this room more than I should. More than any of you deserve. When I tell you that I'm not giving you any of my men, I'm doing it for your own protection. I don't trust my own men. I don't trust any of them, and neither should you," Vincent says.

My mouth gapes. *He's not going to help us. He's just going to leave us all to die.*

He stares at Lennox, exchanging a silent conversation with him.

Lennox stiffens and then gives the slightest nod in agreement.

Gage and Beckett help a moaning Hayes out of the chair, who glares at Vincent as he's helped up. For a minute, I think he's going to have the energy to fight Vincent even in his state, but he says nothing. None of us have anything left to say.

River puts her hand on her stomach protectively. I'm not sure she even realizes she's doing it.

Vincent notices, but it doesn't change his mind. Nothing will.

We ride the elevator down in silence. I have to find a way to protect them. I just don't know how. We walk outside, the high rises towering over us, when a bullet hits Gage.

I scream as I watch him fall to the ground.

My eyes scan the pavement as more bullets fly down upon us. I want to save them. I want to protect them. But I don't have the skills, and I don't know who to try to save.

I spot River, and she's running toward me, away from Beckett.

Fuck, no.

I start running toward her, trying to get her to turn around, to let Beckett protect her and the baby.

But I'm falling to the concrete. The hard, rough surface hits my palms as I catch myself, keeping my face from scraping hard, and then a weight hits me in the back.

I wasn't hit by a bullet.

And I know without looking whose body is covering mine.

Lennox.

"When I tell you, we are going to run toward the car. Don't stop. Don't try to save anyone."

"But—"

"No! For once, trust me that the best way to protect

everyone is to get you out of here. You're the one they want dead," he says into my ear.

I'm not sure how much his words are true or just words to get me to do what he says, but I nod my agreement as more bullets fly close to my head.

"Run," he says, jumping off me, giving me room to run.

I run toward the car, not stopping until I'm in the passenger seat. Lennox jumps into the driver's a second later, and then we're driving before I can even process what happened.

I spot the blood on him. I quickly examine my body, and I realize the blood isn't mine—it's his. He took a bullet for me. *How many of the others did the same?*

CHAPTER 29

Lennox

EVEN THOUGH WE need the extra security, my own apartment feels like a prison now. The entire floor is now being patrolled and guarded by a dozen of Vincent Corsi's best men. After the attack outside his condo, he had no choice but to offer some of his men for protection. And I'm grateful even if I don't like feeling trapped in my own apartment.

Gage took a bullet to the back.

Hayes pulled apart his stitches and bled heavily.

Beckett got a concussion when he hit the pavement, covering Ri with his own body.

Ri, thank goodness, was uninjured—not even a scratch on her body. For added safety, they've moved into an apartment on this floor so we can all be together.

And I took a bullet to my shoulder when I protected Rialta with my own body.

Rialta is beat up. She's scratched and bruised, but it's more than that. It's put her into a dark place. She's barely spoken to anyone. Barely visited Hayes or Gage, who are laid up in bed. Barely left the bedroom.

She just sleeps. And when she's not sleeping, she's sitting in bed and writing in her journal. When I climb into bed at night, she says nothing. She doesn't even fight me. She's become a zombie.

And I have no idea what to do. I still have plenty of time left in the year bargain that I made with Vincent, but every day that she doesn't speak to me feels like a wasted day. And I can't waste any days.

I need her to fall in love with me now. Because I'll never find the snake who attacked us, I know that. Even with the year Vincent gave me, we could all end up dead long before the year is up. And I have to complete my mission before I die.

I'm not sure how to approach her. And I'm not sure if I've made the right decision in asking Vincent to send his men. It gives me time to observe his men and see if I can find a mole in his ranks. And it gives me more men to fight, meaning at least the Retribution Kings will be more cautious in their attacks for the time being.

I stand at the top of the stairs of the loft, waiting for Rialta to notice me. But her head's buried in her journal as she doodles away, completely ignoring me like every other time I've come up here.

I want to talk to her. I want to fuck her again—it's the only time I feel like I have a chance to persuade her that she likes me. But she won't say yes to either of those things. So I approach her with the only thing I know she'll say yes to.

"I'll teach you to fight," I say.

It takes her a second. She's been so used to ignoring me all week; she's not expecting me to say something she might want to respond to.

"What?" She looks up at me, and it takes everything in me not to react to her. She's so pale, her eyes are puffy, and her hair is matted. I don't know when she showered last. All the sleep she's doing isn't helping her—she still looks like she hasn't slept in a month.

"Come to the gym with me. I'll teach you how to fight."

She shakes her head. "I'm a terrible fighter. I always will be. I can't defend myself, let alone anyone else. I can't throw a punch. I have terrible aim with a gun. I can't even run fast enough to shield someone else with my body."

"Well, sulking in bed all day will definitely ensure that you can protect others."

She glares at me.

I grin smugly, loving that I stoked some of that fire within her. She's a spitfire, and as much as she drives me crazy, I'd rather her be fighting with me than ignoring me.

"I'm a good teacher."

"I doubt it."

"Want to make a bet?" I wiggle my eyebrows, knowing her well enough to know she doesn't like to back down from a challenge.

"No, I don't. Last time I made a bet with you, I had to surrender. I won't make that mistake again."

"Is it really so bad to carry one of my babies? I know you'd prefer to carry Kit's baby, but if a child of yours is to have a chance at surviving in this world, it's a good thing to have my genes."

"So the baby can drive me crazy too?"

I laugh at that. "Fine, if you'd rather us spend the day in bed trying to make that baby, then—"

She pops out of the bed before I can finish my sentence. She knows she lost the bet. She knows that I can tell her I want to start trying for a baby, and she'd have to oblige per our deal.

It's not that I want a child. I've never thought of myself as a father. Although, the thought of seeing her stomach growing with my child inside does make me hard and possessive. But then I think how crazy Beckett has been going now that Ri's pregnant, and I think better of it.

But knocking her up would help my relationship with Vincent and his men. With an heir on the way, they'd see that I could fulfill my duties.

Rialta heads to the closet and emerges a few seconds later wearing black leggings and a red sports bra.

Damn.

I chew on my lip, wanting to peel the clothes off her body.

"Get your mind out of the gutter. You're showing me how to fight, remember?"

I pout. "Yes, I remember."

I turn to lead her to the gym when she swipes her journal off the bed. I raise an eyebrow, wondering why she's going to need a journal. *Is she planning on taking notes or something? That's not going to help her.*

"So what are you going to show me? Self-defense? Boxing? How to use a gun?" Rialta asks, putting her journal down on one of the weight benches and then stretching.

I can't take my eyes off her.

I want her—*desperately.*

One time together wasn't enough. I want more. And not because of any arrangement or bet—just for myself.

And then I immediately hate myself for having those thoughts. If I could love her, I'd welcome the dirty thoughts, but my feelings are pure lust.

"No, I'm not going to show you any of those things."

"Why not?"

"For one, my shoulder is still healing, and it's painful to move, let alone physically fight you."

"I'm pretty sure you could still win even with a hurt shoulder. Or are you trying to get me to have some sympathy for you? Because Gage and Hayes suffered far more serious injuries—"

"I'm not looking for sympathy," I cut her off.

She smirks.

"When Hayes is better, you should keep practicing self-defense with him. It will take time to learn and get good enough to actually be able to defend yourself."

"Then, why am I here?"

My eyes darken. "To learn from me. To face your fears."

She frowns, eyeing me suspiciously. "What does that mean?"

"I'm going to find your greatest fears so you can learn to harness them. So you won't be afraid. So when danger comes, you can do something to save yourself."

"You really don't understand me, do you?" She crosses her arms and shakes her head in disappointment.

I walk toward her until we are face to face. "I understand you better than you do."

"I'm not afraid of anything. You forget I've spent my entire life being kidnapped, shot at, and hiding. I spent my entire life looking over my shoulder, wondering if the darkness was going to finally come for me. I'm not afraid of death," she says defiantly.

"I agree, you're not afraid of death." I reach out, caressing her cheek and then lowering my hand to her throat, gripping her as she swallows hard. A glimmer of anxiety flickers in her eyes.

"But you are afraid..."

"There's nothing wrong with being afraid."

"No, there isn't. But there is when you let it control you like you have since we all got shot at. You've been drowning in your own fear."

She swats my hand away from her throat. "I don't let it control me."

"Every decision you've made is out of fear. You gave up Kit because you were afraid of losing him. You ran through a string of bullets because you were afraid of Ri getting hurt. And you're here right now because you're afraid that if you let me fuck you again, you're going to admit how much you like it. How much you like me. How much you want my cock."

"I don't like you. And I don't want your cock. The sex was adequate but not incredible. You tried to scare me then, to make me think you're a villain when you barely tied me up. And any pleasure you heard from me was only because I was pretending you were Kit."

The corner of my lip raises up. "Lies."

She stares at me, trying not to blink or yield, but I know she's lying.

I grab her arm, yanking it behind her back and pulling her to me, so her ass is against my crotch, and she can feel how badly I want her.

Her breathing is hard and fast; her heart is racing.

"You either fear me or want me. Which is it?"

"Neither." She tries to break free of my hold, but I just grab her other wrist and hold them both behind her back with one hand. She's right that even with my hurt shoulder controlling her is easy. She has no skills, no physical ability to save herself.

It's not true. She can save herself. She just has to learn to put herself first and stop being a martyr. But first, she needs to control her fear and learn to think logically.

"I think you fear me," I say, as I run my other hand down the curves of her body from the swell of her breast, over the bare skin of her waist, and then over the tight leggings covering her ass.

"Don't touch me."

"Make me stop."

She tries to break free again but can't.

"I can do anything I want to you."

"No."

"But you can't stop me." I palm her breast in my hand, and the softest of moans leaves her mouth. I know she likes it, but that's not the point. The point is to show her that she can harness her fear. And maybe for her to admit that she craves me as much as I crave her.

"I can. I'll scream if you don't stop."

I chuckle. "Try it. It won't work. The men know I'm alone with you. And mafia men will be happy to know that I'm fucking you against your will. It will make them respect me more."

She screams. It's high-pitched but not truly fearful. *No one will come. No one will save her.*

It's a hard lesson, but one she needs to learn.

After a full minute of screaming, she stops.

"You won't fuck me against my will. You've already proved that you're not a cold-hearted beast."

I laugh. "I'm a cruel fuck; you know that. You've seen what I can do. Maybe I won't fuck you, but I'll push you to your absolute limits, and that's what scares you. Me fucking you against your will would just turn you on. But there are other ways to make you fear me."

She blushes.

I slide my hand down her stomach and under the tight material covering her pussy. My hand slips lower until I find the sweet wetness proving me right.

She sucks in a breath and stills, like if she doesn't move, I won't notice how turned on she is for me.

I drag a finger from her slit to her clit, rubbing the moisture around her already swollen bundle of nerves.

"Fuck," she moans and then gasps as I rub her faster. Her head falls back against my shoulder, but she's not going to get to come until she admits that she wants me. That she wasn't thinking about Kit when I fucked her. That all she thought about was me.

"Admit that all you're thinking about right now is me."

"I'm thinking about Kit."

I remove my hand, leaving her empty and wanting.

Her eyes fly open, and she almost tells me to keep going but stops herself.

So I'll prey on her fear.

I remove my shirt and then tie her wrists together behind her back with it.

"Trying to prove to me that you're kinky? Tying my arms together again won't do that," she teases, but I hear the hint of fear in her voice.

She's afraid, and she needs to learn to control it. If Beckett would let me, I'd tie up Ri and fake doing dirty things to her because I know what Rialta really fears is others getting hurt.

I pull her back to the weight bench, knocking her journal off. I make her straddle the bench, and then I pull her arms back. Then I tie the ends of the shirt to the bar behind her before taking a step back.

Her legs are spread, and her breasts are pushed out, but I want her naked.

I take a knife from my pocket and walk toward her. I hold the knife clearly in front of her, so she has time to anticipate what I'm about to do.

Her chest rises and falls hard, her breasts begging for me.

I take the knife and slip it into the middle of her bra, slicing it open until her breasts spring free. Her hardened nipples pointint directly at me.

I take one in my mouth, teasing it with my tongue as I let the cold blade run down her smooth stomach.

She holds her breath, sucking in her belly to hide from the blade.

I grip the band of her leggings and make a slice.

She gasps.

I continue the rip up her leggings until they're cut open, and her bare pussy is on display for me.

Her eyes dilate, and she licks her lips. I know she wants me. And I want her. But I have far more practice in denying myself than she does. I have more control over my fear too, and I want her to learn to control her fear more than I want to fuck her.

I step back, pick up her journal, and start to walk toward the door.

"What are you doing? Where are you going?"

I turn back, flashing her a vicious grin. "I'm going to let the guys know my wife is tied up and wet and ready to be played with. I'm too hurt to fuck you properly, so I'll offer you to any of them."

"You wouldn't dare," she says.

I shrug. "I don't mind sharing. I've shared before."

Her eyes widen in fear.

I wouldn't dare share her. But she'll worry that I might until I come back to untie her.

"In the meantime, I'll enjoy perusing your journal."

"Don't." Her bottom lip trembles.

"Enjoy your afternoon, wife."

And then I leave her naked, closing the door and taking a seat in front of it. I'm not going to let any of these sick fucks go near her.

I open her journal, and my jaw drops when I see her doodles. My wife has a filthier imagination than I realized. My cock hardens as I look at the little drawings that feature *me*, not Kit. And it takes everything inside me not to go back into that room and fulfill every one of her fantasies.

CHAPTER 30

Rialta

I CAN'T BREATHE.

My pulse is jumping in my throat.

My lip is trembling.

My body is shaking.

I stare at the door.

He left me.

He fucking left me.

My bra has been cut open—same with my leggings.

If anyone walked in, they'd see me naked and tied to this bench. They could do whatever they wanted to me, and I couldn't stop it.

Fucking bastard.

He's too good to rape me, but he has no problem letting others do it. *It's the same damn thing!*

He's shared before. What does that mean? Did Hayes and Gage use to share girls with him?

It's kind of hot if it's true.

But I can't think about that now. I have to figure out how to stop this because while I might be okay with Hayes and Gage fucking me—the others...I wouldn't survive.

I know that now.

I used to think I'd be strong enough to survive being violated, but it hasn't even happened yet, and I know I'm wrong.

I can't think as my body floods with warmth. I don't know why Lennox did this. *Does he hate me that much? Is he that upset that I said I was thinking about Kit when we fucked?*

Because god, it wasn't true.

Every second with Lennox felt like a betrayal to Kit. Even though I ended things with Kit and then ensured he saw what I did so he'd hate me. I did it so he wouldn't hope. So he would never be willing to take me back. So that chapter of my life would be closed and could never be opened again. I did it to let Kit go, to stop our hearts from wishing.

But when it came down to it, I only thought of Lennox when I was with him. And as much as I loved Kit, Lennox is the one I fantasize about fucking again.

And now he has proof of that—he has my journal.

Fuck, that strikes more fear in me than being tied up. When I haven't been thinking about how so many people I care about are at risk of dying because of me these last few days, my mind has been fantasizing about being tied up, spanked, and degraded by Lennox. It's the only thing that can pull me away from my painful thoughts.

I start breathing faster, my eyes never tearing from the door. With each second that passes, it makes me think it's not a sick joke. I realize he isn't going to just open the door and come back in and untie me or fuck me.

My breathing is quick and shallow. I'm not getting enough oxygen, which is only making things worse. My heart is beating out of my chest. I flinch at every sound I hear outside the door. Any second, the door will open, and a monster will come in.

Fuck Lennox. Fuck him.

When I get out of here, I'm going to kill him. I don't care about the consequences. I don't care that Vincent will only make me marry again, and the next man could be worse. I—

I stare at the door.

And it hits me all at once.

Just like before.

Lennox is protecting me.

But this time, he's doing it with a lesson—a ruthless lesson.

No one is coming in.

No one is going to hurt me.

No one is going to touch me.

I take a deep breath. Then another and another.

I feel my pulse slowing. My body calms as I get more and more oxygen.

I can control my fear. I've always been able to control my fear. I had forgotten.

My shoulders relax as that thought creeps in.

I can control my fear.

I can't control what happens to me. I can't control what happens to others, but I can control how I react.

I'm not afraid of death or pain. And all those bodily reactions were as much about being turned on by Lennox as it was about fear. And even if my body reacts to the fear, I still have control of my mind.

I wiggle my arms against the fabric and am able to inch my wrist up.

And I can get free.

I take my time, thinking about how I can get my arms

loose. I wiggle and move my wrists methodically until I slip one free.

I grin.

I did it.

Once both arms are free, I get off the bench, looking immediately for something to cover my nakedness with.

All the while, I can't stop smiling. I can't stop feeling like I can survive anything.

Lennox.

I pause.

I hate him.

I want him.

Could I learn to love him?

He taught me more in one lesson than Hayes could in a month. It was brutal and harsh. But he knows how stubborn and determined to get in my own way I am. And he knows how I desperately need to be reminded that I can save myself. That I'm strong. That I can't always fight back with my fists, but if I can calm my mind, I can find a way to save myself or, more importantly, others.

I find a towel and wrap it around myself before heading out. I don't know what to do about Lennox, but first things first, I need to go back to our apartment and get dressed.

And I need to get my journal back.

I open the door, and Lennox falls back, my journal in his hand.

He's been leaning against the door this whole time, ensuring no one touches me.

I smirk at that.

And then I realize exactly how I'm going to handle him.

I drop the towel.

And Lennox sits up quickly.

"That was fast," he says.

"I'm a fast learner. Thanks for the lesson." I strut past him, almost completely naked.

Lennox is shocked. Shocked that I didn't fight with him, that I thanked him.

And now he's shocked that I'm not covering myself up in front of the dozen men in the hallway.

"Keep your eyes off my wife if you don't want to end up dead," Lennox growls down the hallway.

The men's eyes flicker upward, but not before they all get an eyeful of my body.

I can hear Lennox growling his discontent with me as I walk to our apartment.

Serves him right for the harsh lesson. I'm not going to let him win our battles without a little bit of retribution, even if I'm starting to enjoy them immensely.

CHAPTER 31

Lennox

"THERE HAVE BEEN NO MORE ATTACKS?" Vincent Corsi asks.

"None, sir," I say into my phone while I pace outside of Hayes's room. Gage has healed well and has been sleeping on the floor next to Hayes's bed. While Hayes has been taking a longer time to heal. Probably because he keeps trying to push himself and then reopens his stitches. If he'd just stay in bed, he'd be healed by now. Which is why Gage is now sleeping on the floor to ensure he stays in bed instead of trying to cook for everyone or cheer everyone up.

"Good." There's a pause as if he's deciding if he should tell me the next part or not. But then he says, "Be ready for anything."

"What do you mean? Do you know something?"

"I just know my men. They don't feel like I've sufficiently tested you yet. They aren't happy with our arrangement when they've worked for me their whole lives, and I've only known you for a few weeks. They think you'll fail. And they want you to fail sooner rather than later."

I frown, although I already knew that's what I was

risking by inviting them here. But I had no choice, especially after the latest attack. The only reason we haven't been attacked again is because of them. If we weren't protected, anyone who was watching us would know Hayes, Gage, and Beckett were injured. Ri is pregnant, and Rialta can't protect herself.

If it wasn't for them, we'd all be dead by now.

But it is strange that the men haven't tried their own shenanigans. They haven't tested my authority at all. For the most part, they've done exactly as I've asked. I know that it can't last, though.

"Thanks for the warning, but I'm prepared to handle any tests from your men."

"See that you are." And then the phone call ends.

I pocket my phone as I check in on Gage and Hayes. Hayes is sleeping for once, and Gage shoos me out. It's not the time to talk to them.

I step back out of their room and then text Gage to be ready for anything.

I walk the short distance down the hallway back to my apartment, and I feel the gaze of every man on guard in the hallway. Almost all look like they'd rather kill me than protect me. I know the feeling. I don't trust any of them, either.

"Are you in charge, or is she?" Andrea says, blocking the door to my apartment.

I've made it a goal to learn all of their names as quickly as possible. Gage has been sending me reports on all of them. Andrea is young but has raced up the ranks quickly, mainly by challenging his superior and then gaining the support of the others. Vincent didn't care about infighting as long as his orders were followed, but I'm wondering if that was a mistake.

"You dare to question my authority?" I say.

Andrea squares his shoulders. "Yes, I think you are pathetic. I don't think you're ready to become a crime lord. You can't even control Rialta. And you were kicked out of the Retribution Kings. You won't last the year."

He's probably right. I don't expect to last the year. But I'm not going to tell him that.

If I was Vincent, I would kill him or punish him for disobeying me. But I'm not Vincent. I'm the heir, not the king yet. And if I were to kill one of Vincent's best men without talking to him first, he'd probably kill me. Plus, sure, it would make the others fear me, but they wouldn't respect me. It would only make them hate me more.

I need a move that would make them respect me like they respect Vincent. I just don't know what that is yet.

I keep my cool. I don't let Andrea shake me.

Instead, I smirk slowly and deliberately.

"And you think you should be the heir?"

He grins viciously. "Yes, I've earned it."

I nod and step toward him.

He flinches ever so slightly, assuming I'm going to hit him. Shoot him. Kill him.

But I'm not Vincent.

I grab the door handle behind him and push the door open to my apartment.

I shove Andrea out of my way, and then I yell out, "Rialta, come here."

I don't add, please, and I don't ask her. I tell her.

It's a risky move, but I know Rialta won't fail me. Call it a gut feeling.

Rialta strolls through the door a second later.

"Andrea here thinks he should be Vincent's heir instead of me. He should be your husband instead of me. What do you think of that?"

She looks at me cautiously as she stands in her black

leggings and an oversized cream-colored sweatshirt. Her hair is tied up in a messy bun on top of her head, and somehow she's sexy without even trying.

My cock is already straining toward her—wanting her desperately.

I fold my arms, telling her I trust her to handle this as my smirk grows larger.

Her eyes cut from me to him. She lets her eyes go up and down his body, assessing him. She takes her time examining him—from his tight dark jeans, to his fitted dark shirt, to the tattoos creeping out from his biceps down his arms. She studies every part of his body except his face. When her eyes finally meet his, she says, "Hmm, I think you're too small to be a mafia boss." Her eyes cut to his crotch. "And definitely too small to be my husband."

The other guys watching snicker, and my eyes heat. I love seeing her sassy mouth being used to take down someone other than me.

"I'm plenty big enough, sweetheart—" He grabs her ass.

She slaps him hard across the cheek, and then I yank her to me. I growl at him before punching him right where she slapped him, knocking him on his ass.

"Touch what's mine again without my permission, and it will be the last thing you do," I say.

His face flushes red, and the guys in the hallway laugh.

I pull Rialta tighter against me, wrapping my arm possessively around her waist as we walk into the apartment together. The second I shut the door behind us, she lets out a long breath, like she's been holding it the entire time. Her head rests on my shoulder like she needs me to stay close.

I don't let go of her, giving her time to take in what just happened.

"You did well," I say.

She nods against my chest, and then she looks up at me. "It's going to get worse, isn't it?"

"Probably."

She nods again.

It's all going to get worse. The men testing me. The Retribution Kings attacking. And the man who will hunt her to the end of the earth will eventually kill her and me—if her father and his men don't do it first.

"Get me pregnant," she says.

I blink, not sure I heard her correctly.

"That will at least fix one problem. The Corsi men will respect you if you knock me up, and I'm carrying the next heir. They'll have to. It won't solve all of our problems, but it will at least solve one."

She's right, but I know she doesn't want to get pregnant. That's why she made the bet with me.

And I don't really care if I get her pregnant or not. A child is the last thing on my mind. Any child of mine would be fatherless, and that seems like a cruel thing to do to someone so innocent.

But I realize what she's doing by telling me to get her pregnant. She's telling me that I'm her future. That she's accepted her fate. And if the heat in her eyes is anything to go by—she's telling me that she wants me to fuck her, but she's too scared to ask outright.

"If you want me to fuck you, wife, all you have to do is ask," I purr.

She swallows hard. "Husband, will you please fuck me?"

CHAPTER 32

Rialta

LENNOX LIKES it when I beg. I can see how his eyes darken, and his cock hardens beneath his jeans when I beg him to fuck me—my voice sweet and sultry as I ask.

It turns me on, too, although I don't want to admit it. I don't want to want him.

And yet I do.

I want him so fucking badly; I'm willing to chance getting pregnant with his baby.

God, that thought is a lot.

It would solve the problem of the men trusting our relationship. I know half the men think he's a mole placed here by the Retribution Kings, and the other half think he's incompetent and hasn't earned it yet.

A baby would change things.

His tongue licks over his bottom lip as he stares at me in my ratty clothes and bare face. I didn't bother putting on makeup or real clothes, preferring to be comfy. But I wish I had made more of an effort. Because if he's looking at me like this in these clothes, I'm dying to know how he'd look at me in something sexier.

"Gladly, my wife. I'll fuck you however you want. In any position you want. Perhaps one of those fantasies you wrote down in your journal?" I can see the excitement and lust in his eyes at the thought of acting out one of my fantasies.

My cheeks heat, and my hands tremble, but I'm not ready. Not ready to give in to my feelings completely. And I'm too embarrassed to articulate any of them.

"No," I say, unable to say more.

He nods, but there is no disappointment on his face. In fact, I think I see his face light up even more with lust as he stares at me.

I bite my lip, not sure what's going to happen now. *Is he still going to fuck me?*

He takes a step forward, and I gulp, anticipating what's going to happen next. But when it comes to Lennox, I'm clueless.

He holds out his hand to me, and I hesitantly take it, prepared to be tied up, to be spanked, to be degraded. I want him to do that. I want dangerous, unpredictable, passionate sex. I want to try everything imaginable with him. Everything I never dreamed about with Kit.

But—Lennox doesn't say a word. He just leads me upstairs to the bed loft, and then he lets go of my hand.

I'm standing at the foot of the bed, watching Lennox closely. He moves like he isn't injured. If he feels the pain, he doesn't react to it. And he punched Andrea with the same arm that took a bullet a week ago. He either has no nerve endings, or he's found a way to block out the pain. He's not fully healed if the others are anything to go by.

He pulls off his shirt, his muscles rippling. The bandage over his right shoulder, proving my point, is blood-soaked.

He stares at me, and my eyes are quickly drawn south as he undoes his jeans and pushes them and his briefs down in one movement.

My eyes widen, and a smile spreads over my face at the sight of him. He's so beautiful, with his tattoos covering almost every inch of him. His skin glued over his bulging muscles. And that dark glare that's meant to intimidate, but it just makes me want him more.

It's almost enough to get me to articulate my wicked desires out loud, but he beats me to it. He falls back on the bed.

"Ride me, wife. Show me how much you like my cock."

I nod.

And then I rip off my sweatshirt, exposing my breasts to him.

His jaw twitches at the sight, but he doesn't move. He's patient.

I'm not.

My leggings and thong go next, and then I'm racing up the bed, fumbling over his legs as I come face-to-face with the head of his cock.

"Lick it, wife," he growls.

"No."

He frowns, but before he can get a snarky command off, I have his cock down my throat.

He gasps.

And now I'm the one smirking around his cock as I suck him deeper and deeper down my throat until I can't take him any further.

He groans every time my lips slide up and down his cock, but I refuse to lick him. I refuse to let him feel the wetness of my tongue, and I know it's driving him mad.

He fists my hair, yanking me off suddenly. "You're going to pay for that, my dear wife. Soon you're going to beg for me to fulfill those fantasies of yours. And when you do, I'll enjoy punishing you for every disobedient action you do now."

I'm drenched at that thought. "That doesn't give me any incentive to obey then," I purr.

"God, you're incredible and infuriating at the same time."

"Ditto."

And then I climb up his body until I'm straddling him —his cock pushing between my thighs.

Our eyes meet.

Reality hits us.

And before either of us can decide to stop, I slide my hips down over his cock, and he slides inside me. The burn hits me, but I don't stop.

Lennox leans forward, capturing my lips, and the pain is gone.

I grip his shoulders as I start riding him, and he continues the kiss.

And then I realize I'm gripping the shoulder that was shot. I try to remove my hand, but Lennox stops me with a thrust, forcing me to grip him to keep from falling off him.

"Fuck me, wife," he growls against my lips before nipping them.

The light taste of metal enters my mouth from where he nicked me. It's like fire burning through my body. I crave more.

I fuck him—hard.

I ride him for as long as we both can stand it. Until we're sweaty and exhausted and can do nothing except pour our orgasms into the other.

We fuck without a condom.

We could get pregnant.

Or we could die first.

Or...

Or I could fall in love with the devil.

CHAPTER 33

Lennox

I STARTLE AWAKE to darkness being pulled over my face, when moments before I was stroking Rialta's hair as she was tucked into the crook of my arm.

I'm dragged from the bed.

I don't have time to reach for the gun in my nightstand.

I don't have time to grab Rialta.

I don't have time to get a punch in.

I'm completely fucking useless.

My arms are handcuffed behind my back. The hood covering my face is tightened so I can't see shit. And I can feel a gun pointed at my back.

The only thing I can do is breathe and hope that I have time.

I have to have time left.

This can't be the end.

I need more time.

Rialta.

I listen carefully, trying to listen to any sounds of what she's doing. But I can't hear her. I can't hear anything but the shuffling of feet.

Fuck, what happened?

Did the Retribution Kings attack?

Did the man who wants Rialta dead attack?

Neither seems likely with the Corsi men constantly guarding us.

Andrea.

He's behind this.

I don't understand why yet, but he would be the only one with access and a grudge after what happened last night. Vincent Corsi warned me this would happen. Now I just have to figure out how to stay alive.

It's a test.

A test that, if I fail, will end in my death.

I'm pulled through the hallways of the apartment building and down a set of stairs. It takes all of my energy to keep up and not trip on the steps.

When a cool evening breeze hits my bare skin, I realize I'm still naked. I'm going to kill them after this is over.

I'm tossed into the back of a van. I wait for Rialta to be thrown in next to me. But as the van starts moving, I realize I'm alone.

My heart thunders in my chest. *Where the fuck are they taking Rialta?*

I struggle against the handcuffs that I know I won't be able to get out of. I consider kicking the door open and jumping out, but I still think my best chance of finding Rialta is letting them take me where they want to take me. Even though she's not in the same van, I still think she's headed to the same place I am. Andrea will want her to see me humiliated. He'll keep her alive. Vincent will kill him if he kills Rialta. But I don't know if it will stop him from touching her, hurting her.

I grind my teeth together, frustrated with myself for

being so foolish. I should have never trusted any of them. Now I endangered everyone.

The van stops, and I'm pulled out.

I force my legs to keep going so I don't stumble as I walk. I need to keep as much of my pride as I can.

We head down a set of stairs as more cool air hits me.

And then the hood is removed from my head, and every thought I had is confirmed in a second.

Andrea is behind this. And he got every man who was supposed to be protecting us to follow him. I count every single one in the basement.

Hayes, Gage, Beckett, and Ri are, thankfully, absent.

But my eyes immediately go to Rialta Corsi, standing next to Andrea as he holds onto her wrist.

I examine her quickly from where I stand naked and handcuffed across the dank basement that we've been brought to. She doesn't look hurt, and she's at least wearing clothes—the same leggings and sweatshirt that she tore off her body last night before she fucked me.

"You have failed, Lennox. It's time to end things before we end you," Andrea says.

I laugh maniacally. "I failed? You're the one who kidnapped the heir and his wife. You're the one who failed."

Andrea shakes his head. "I'm not the one handcuffed naked with guns pointed at my head. That would be you."

"Don't worry; I'll rectify that soon enough." I glare at him. The tick in his jaw tells me he sees what I plan to do to him as soon as I'm free. He better kill me tonight, along with everyone else on my team, or this will cost him his life. I'll find a way to kill him even if I'm dead.

"I doubt that when you can't even fulfill your most basic duties." Andrea turns to Rialta. "You've failed as a husband. Rialta ran off last night. She didn't want to be with you."

I look from him to Rialta. Her eyes widen.

Andrea is lying.

She wouldn't run away. She has before, but she wouldn't again. Not unless there was a very good reason, but even then—she'd have woken me up or told one of the others. And after our fuck last night, I know she wouldn't just leave my bed willingly.

"You failed to keep her satisfied. You failed to protect her. And you proved how pathetic of a mob boss you would be when you could be so easily captured," he continues.

I glare at him but don't say anything because he's right. I failed. Even though I was counting on them to help us, I should have been prepared for this.

I look at Rialta—I should have prepared her for this too. She must be terrified.

I look her in the eyes, trying to comfort her, even though I don't have a way out of this that keeps us both alive. But I find no fear. She looks at me with a dark gleam that says she's ready to fight.

That's my girl. I knew she had it in her; it just needed to be coaxed out of her.

"You shouldn't be the heir. Divorce her and leave, and we'll let you live," Andrea continues.

The rest of the men are silent, just watching the exchange. Andrea thinks he's won them—that they're all on his side. But the silence tells me they are here just to watch the show. They won't fully pledge me their loyalty until I complete my deal with Vincent and take over his job.

I still have time to win them to my side. Andrea won't kill me tonight; I won't let him.

"You know I won't do that."

Andrea snickers, like I just walked into his trap. "We can't kill you per the arrangement you made with Vincent. But you can prove to us that you are worthy of the job. Punish your wife for leaving so she never puts us in danger again. Convince us you have control of her. Maybe we'll let you walk out of here with the arrangement still intact. Otherwise, we might just kill you and face Vincent's wrath."

He nods at Logan, the man standing to my right. He walks behind me and unlocks the handcuffs—releasing me.

This is about embarrassing me.

This is about degrading her and making her hate me.

This is about reducing my authority.

I consider my options.

Refuse and fight—and end up dead. Even if I was completely healthy and had a weapon, I couldn't take on over a dozen men with guns and make it out alive.

Convince Andrea to stop this—very unlikely.

Or surrender—and fight to live another day. But it would mean hurting Rialta, and that's not something I'm willing to do at the moment.

I remain calm as I think through the choices. I've been in worse situations before and survived them. But I can't find a way to get out of this.

Until I look at Rialta.

She rakes her teeth over her bottom lip.

My eyes widen.

She can't be offering...

And then she winks at me with a twinkle in her eye. And I know exactly what I'm going to do.

"Oh, I'll punish her."

And when I'm finished punishing her, I'm going to punish all of you. And unlike her, you're not going to like it.

CHAPTER 34

Rialta

ANDREA IS A FUCKING LIAR, and I'm going to kill him if Lennox doesn't. He woke me in the middle of the night from Lennox's bed and told me Vincent was on the phone waiting for me.

Next thing I know, I passed out and woke up here, listening to Andrea tell me he thinks Lennox is still a Retribution King. Lennox only sees me as property, he can't protect me, and he's an abuser. He said Lennox will only hurt me.

Lie after lie after lie.

Andrea told me what's about to happen is a test, and that Lennox will have to face many tests if he wants to stay Vincent's successor. If he passes, I will have a better bond with Lennox, but he doesn't think he'll pass. He said I should be prepared to divorce him, to not get too attached. He'll most likely be dead within the month if he fails.

I want to fight.

I want to tell Andrea how wrong he is.

I want to kick him in the balls.

But I do none of those things. I keep a blank, shocked expression. I don't let Andrea know whose side I'm on. I can't let him know how I feel.

I play the long game. I don't know when this ends, but it doesn't end tonight. Lennox will survive whatever test is placed in front of him. And if Andrea thinks he can convince me to leave Lennox, then I can use that to my advantage and extract information from him to learn what he's scheming.

But when I saw Lennox dragged into the dungy basement—naked and handcuffed—I almost broke. Yet, somehow even as he stood naked before everyone, Lennox looked like the most menacing man here.

He didn't look afraid. He looked powerful and mine.

Fuck, Lennox is mine.

I can't lose him.

I don't know when I started thinking of him in that way. And it doesn't change how I felt about Kit. But Kit was the sweet crush who taught me how to make love. Lennox is the bad boy asshole I want to teach me how to fuck. Both are mine in very different ways. Both of them I'll protect with my life.

I've already protected Kit. Now it's time to protect Lennox.

I can't let Lennox die. Andrea spoke of an arrangement Lennox has with Vincent that prevents him from killing him now, but I doubt that will stop him if he doesn't get what he wants from Lennox—which is to put a wedge between us. To make me hate Lennox. To get me to call Vincent immediately when I leave here and demand a divorce.

Punish me—that's what Andrea said he wanted Lennox to do.

I wink at Lennox. I'm a-okay with Lennox punishing

me. He's read my journal. He knows what I fantasize about. And I trust him to punish me in a way that I'll enjoy. Lennox understands me better than I understand myself. He proved it when he reminded me how strong I am, how to wield my strength.

I trust him.

Lennox glares around the room. His eyes tell every man in the room that if they don't eventually bow to him, they'll soon be buried six feet under.

I follow his gaze around the room, and it seems that most of them get the message. But it's not enough for them to put a stop to this.

Andrea pushes me forward, and Lennox growls at him. It echoes through the room.

Everyone stops breathing as Lennox speaks like he's possessed by the devil himself, "Don't. Touch. My. Wife. Ever. Again."

Andrea just smiles. "I will if she still wants to remain your wife after tonight."

I fist my hands at my side to keep from turning and throwing a punch at Andrea. He's just trying to show that Lennox is too weak to fight back, that he can't protect me.

Andrea doesn't realize that Lennox is my fucked up villain. I've barely gotten to see his dark side, but I've gotten a tiny taste, and now I want more.

Andrea doesn't know that I'm as fucked up as Lennox is. I crave being defiled, and I have a very dark fantasy about being fucked in front of others. I need to be told I'm his and no one else's.

Lennox looks to me and points at a spot on the floor in front of him. "On your knees, wife."

I take a deep breath and step forward with trembling legs. I'm not afraid of Lennox hurting me, but I am afraid that my fantasies are just that—fantasies. Maybe they aren't something I'd actually enjoy. Maybe he's going to push me beyond the limits of my fantasies, beyond what I'm comfortable with—whatever that line is. I haven't tested it yet, so I have no clue. And I wish this wasn't the first test of those limits.

I walk until I'm right in front of Lennox and kneel on the dirt-covered floor, my eyes looking up at him as his cock strains in my direction.

"Suck me, wife. Show these men you're mine and no one else's. Show them how good you suck my dick but will never touch theirs."

I feel my body tremble, rumbling from the inside out.

Lennox's eyes are on me and filled with lust. His cock is hard and yearning for me. He doesn't give a damn about any of the men watching us.

I lick my lips. I don't, either. I just want him to feel good. I wrap my lips around his cock and suck.

"Good girl."

I smile and suck him harder, my lips sliding over his hard cock. My hand comes up to stroke him, but he grabs my hand before I can reach him.

"Only use your mouth and take me all the way."

He's gripping my wrist tightly, but it feels like he's doing it to keep his control more than anything. I can't tell if he's trying to keep from attacking Andrea or from coming down my throat too fast.

I suck him hungrily. He hits the back of my throat, and I gag.

Lennox groans.

Then Andrea clears his throat, bringing me back to the realization that I have an audience.

My cheeks flush bright red.

Lennox grabs a handful of my hair into a ponytail at the back of my head and pulls me off his cock.

"You're mine. I'm going to paint your ass red so you can't sit down for a week, so you won't be able to run from me. And then I'm going to make you come so fucking hard that everyone within a mile will hear you and know that YOU'RE MINE."

I'm panting.

It's exactly how I described it in my journal.

He remembered.

But panic is also beating through me.

I want to be spanked. I want to feel his hand against my ass. I want to feel like he owns me, controls me. I want to see what that freedom is like to willingly surrender to someone else.

And yet, Andrea is here. Men my father's age are here.

Lennox doesn't seem to mind his nakedness in front of them. But I'm blushing, and I'm still fully dressed.

I can't.

My eyes are wild with fear.

And I hear a couple of the men chuckle.

I cast my eyes down in disgrace.

I can't do this.

Lennox is going to die.

Fuck.

I have to do this—I can't—I can—I can't—

I feel his finger under my chin, tilting it up so I'm looking only at him. His eyes are pure evil. His grimace is unyielding. His nostrils flare with malice.

But his touch—that single touch is a warm and firm directive.

He doesn't speak.

He's giving me a chance to back out, to change my

mind. I'm in control of the decision. I'm in control if he lives tonight or dies.

And I already know my answer, even if it breaks me. I take a deep breath, pursing my lips as I slowly exhale.

Lennox gives me a tight nod.

He won't break me.

This won't break me.

"Turn around on all fours," Lennox says deeply, his voice music to my heart, making my core pulse with desire.

I don't care what he does to me.

I don't care who sees.

I'm soaked with need at how he lets me decide—but when I do, I'm his completely.

I turn around on all fours, and I'm looking directly at Andrea.

At first, I want to spin around and tell Lennox how horrible of an idea this is, but then I feel Lennox's hand on my ass—he rubs his palm in a slow circle over my leggings, promising to fulfill my dark desires.

"I'm going to spank you, and then I'm going to make you come, wife. I'm going to break you apart for everyone to see."

And then, without warning, he lowers my leggings and spanks me hard.

I yelp as the sting spreads through me and flushes my entire body. I feel the vibration from my ass to my lips. If I wasn't wet already, I am now.

"Tell me you're sorry."

"I'm sorry," I whisper.

"Louder."

"I'm sorry!" I shout.

His hand comes down on my ass again, harder than the previous time, and I whimper.

"Tell me you'll never leave again without my permission."

"I'll never leave again without your permission."

Another slap.

My body jerks forward, and my whimper turns into a cry.

I look up at Andrea, who is smirking down at me.

"Tell me you're mine."

He slaps me again so hard that tears well in my eyes as I stare at Andrea.

He thinks he's won—Lennox broke me. *What a fool Andrea is.*

Lennox just made me feel powerful. He just fulfilled a fantasy.

"Tell me you're mine." The slap rings through the room.

I lick my lips as tears fall and my pussy wets in equal measure.

"I'm yours," I groan.

And then his hand is between my legs.

Two fingers push into my slit, another at my clit.

I gasp.

My back arches.

My mouth opens.

Every part of me capitulates to him.

I am his.

I feel him everywhere.

The pain.

The pleasure.

The intensity of the onlooking stares as they watch such an intimate act.

It all swirls and forms into a hurricane taking over the room.

Andrea grins.

He truly doesn't realize what's happening.

But Lennox does.

And I do.

"Come, my dirty, filthy wife. Come and show them how I command your body. How I control you. How you're fucking mine."

I come and see stars—I see a future.

I come screaming Lennox's name in a room full of vile, dangerous men.

And it's the hottest fucking thing Lennox, or any man, has done to me.

I want more.

More filth.

More danger.

More desire.

But I need to find the truth. Lennox can't keep me in the dark. He can't keep hiding the truth from me.

I need to know the truth of the deal he struck with Vincent. I need to know all his secrets.

I want to know everything about Lennox Corsi—the man who is wickedness himself. A man who is darkness, and desires, and death. A man who has given more than he's ever taken. A man who has hidden so much from me, and yet I get glimpses of the real man behind his grumpy facade and the pain he's endured.

I could love him.

The kind of love that is greater than anything else. The kind that endures. The kind that can as easily end in forever like Noah and Allie or tragedy like Romeo and Juliet. Our love is all that matters.

It terrifies me.

Loving Kit was like loving a gentle summer breeze—easy and calm. Loving Lennox is like loving a hurricane—it's all-consuming.

I don't love him yet.

I can't love him.

Not until I know him.

Not until I've heard every truth.

Every secret.

Every bit of darkness in his soul and he mine.

And I will learn his secrets. It's the only way we'll all stay alive.

CHAPTER 35

Rialta

"I'M SORRY," Lennox says as he slams the door shut back in his apartment.

He's still naked, and I'm still aching from Lennox's touch.

He walks over to the couch and wraps a throw blanket around his waist so he's somewhat covered.

"I'm not. We survived; that's all that matters. Plus..." I blush. "That was, uh..."

I can't bring myself to say the rest. I have no problem arguing with the man and telling him everything on my mind, but when it comes to my sexual desires, I just can't say them out loud to him. I'm not ashamed of them. I'm just not sure of my own feelings yet.

He smirks. "You're not sorry for the best fucking orgasm of your life or for fulfilling your sexual fantasy from your journal that I would have satisfied at some point anyway?"

I tuck a strand of my hair behind my ear and nod with a soft smile. The experience would have been perfect if we weren't having to do it because of Andrea. If we had chosen to play that game, it would have been exactly what I'd fantasized.

"I'm sorry I let Andrea take you. I'm sorry I couldn't keep you safe."

I frown. "It's not your fault."

He shakes his head. "It is my fault. As much as I wish I could promise I could keep you safe—I can't. I can't make that promise and keep it. We have too many enemies, you and I. Too many people that want us dead."

"You don't need to apologize for that. I've lived my entire life with people trying to keep me safe. I've always known I'll die young. Dying doesn't stop me from living."

"No, it doesn't." He reaches his hand out and strokes my cheek.

I close my eyes, loving his gentle touch on my face. All I want is to curl up in bed with him, have him wrap his arms and legs around me, and sleep.

It's not Lennox's style, though. We've only ever cuddled post-sex. But I'm too tired to fuck tonight. And from the looks of Lennox, he's too tired too.

I open my eyes. There is one conversation that we need to have before we sleep.

"What is the deal you made with my father?" My eyes are serious as I look into Lennox's, telling him I won't take no for an answer.

Lennox drops his hand from my face. "Trust me when I tell you it's best you don't know."

"Why? After everything we've been through tonight alone, don't you think I deserve to know? Don't you think if I knew, I could help you? Don't you trust me?"

"I trust you, Rialta. But I'm asking that you trust me." His voice breaks into a deep sadness as he says it.

"Why? Why is it so important that I don't know?"

"It's not your burden to bear. It's mine."

"You can tell me," I whisper. *I think I'm falling in love with you if you'd just let me in.*

He sighs. "I'll tell you when the time is right. I will tell you. I promise you that. Is that enough for you?"

No, it's not enough, but that's not what I say. I say the only thing I can muster. "Okay."

"Beckett, Ri, Gage, and Hayes are going to take turns guarding the apartment while Corsi's men patrol the hallways. I can't dismiss them, and we still need their protection if the Retribution Kings or your unknown enemy attacks, but our team can at least ensure we don't get kidnapped by our own men again."

"Are any of them healed enough? And River shouldn't help in her condition—"

"I know, I don't like it either. But I've instructed them to take turns hanging on the couch and watching the cameras. We just want someone awake who can warn us if anyone tries to enter. I'm not asking them to fight for us."

I nod.

And then I hear a knock as if whoever it is was listening to our conversation.

Lennox opens the door, and River and Beckett come inside. River runs to me, wrapping her arms around me.

"I'm so sorry, I—"

"Stop it. You have nothing to apologize for."

I feel River's tears drop down onto my shoulder. "It's my job to protect you, and I failed. Now that I'm pregnant—"

"Now that you're pregnant, it's your job to protect that baby. It's Lennox's job to protect me." I look at her sternly. "Sleep on the couch. Beckett will watch the cameras. And if anyone comes, go to the safe room in the closet upstairs, understand?"

River frowns. "But—"

"That's exactly what you'll do," Lennox says.

Beckett also gives River a stern look, needing his wife to take it easy.

She pouts but then rubs her belly, and I know she'll do anything to protect her baby. And then she yawns, which sets off a string of yawns through the room.

"Get to bed," River says.

"Are you going to be comfortable on the couch? If not, you can—"

"I can fall asleep anywhere now that I'm pregnant," River chuckles, interrupting me.

We hug, and then I climb the stairs with Lennox behind me. I sit on the edge of the bed to remove my shoes and wince.

Lennox frowns and heads to the bathroom while I remove my shoes.

"Remove your leggings and tell me where it hurts," he says, holding a cream and a cool washcloth in his hand.

I blush. "It's sweet of you, but it doesn't hurt that bad."

"I don't care if it hurts a little or a lot; I want to take care of you."

"You're far more hurt than I am, and you don't let me take care of you." I motion to his shoulder.

"That's because I don't feel pain."

I frown. "Of course—"

He motions to his shoulder. "It doesn't hurt at all. Trust me."

I want to ask more questions, but I yawn and decide it will have to wait for tomorrow.

Lennox helps me undress—pulling the sweatshirt over my head and then very slowly peeling my leggings from my body as I try not to wince.

It does sting.

"Lay down on the bed," he commands.

I lay on my stomach and feel the bed dip as Lennox

climbs in next to me. Then he gently rubs cream on my sore ass.

I moan quietly.

"If you keep doing that, I'm going to fuck you. And I don't think you want that, considering your sister and brother-in-law are downstairs and could hear everything. And your ass is far too sore for what I want to do to you," he hisses in my ear.

"Then stop rubbing me and hold me."

He immediately does. His arms drape over me protectively, and I know the second I close my eyes, I'll sleep peacefully through the night.

———

I wake up drenched in sweat and sick to my stomach. Lennox's arm is draped over my waist, and it's still dark out.

I jump up out of bed and race to the bathroom, making it to the toilet just in time to vomit the contents of my stomach.

A second later, I feel Lennox's hand on my back, rubbing gently.

"I get nightmares too. I can't tell you they'll go away anytime soon, but the physical reaction you feel usually goes away after a while," he says.

I nod, but it wasn't a nightmare. I feel physically ill.

No...

No.

No.

No.

No, no, no.

No—it can't be.

"Rialta, are you okay? It looks like you've seen a ghost," Lennox says, rubbing his hand over my forehead.

I give him the smallest smile I can force on my face.

"You don't feel hot."

"It was just a nightmare," I say, but I'm still lost in my own thoughts. Even though I know it's true, I can't help but do mental math, searching for proof to make it impossible.

I assess my body—my breasts feel sore, I'm exhausted, bloated, sick...and most importantly, I've missed my period.

But if I'm pregnant, it wouldn't be Lennox's. It would be...

FUCK.

How could I have been so stupid?

And what the hell am I going to do about it?

I should take a test, but I don't need a test to tell me I'm pregnant.

"Hey, are you okay?" Hayes asks from the doorway.

We both look in his direction. He looks good. If I didn't know he'd been shot, then I wouldn't know.

"Yea, just a nightmare," I say weakly.

Hayes looks at me with concern and then to Lennox, who is still rubbing my back.

"Want anything to eat?" Hayes asks.

My stomach lights up at the thought of food. "Yea, I'd like that."

Lennox helps me stand up, and it's then that I realize we are both naked.

"Get out of here and stop looking at my wife that way. I'll send her down when she's dressed to eat," Lennox says.

Hayes flashes a crooked grin, and then he's gone.

"It's good to see Hayes back to his usual self," I say, trying to take my mind off the fact that I'm most likely pregnant with the wrong man's baby.

"It is," Lennox agrees.

I get dressed in one of Lennox's shirts and a loose pair of my own shorts. Lennox puts on a pair of his boxer briefs.

"You can go back to bed. Hayes will take care of me," I say.

Lennox groans.

I chuckle. "I'm fine, and I'll make sure Hayes doesn't kiss me again."

Lennox licks his lips, then leans in and kisses me. It's such a casual thing, the kind of thing real couples do—not enemies in arranged marriages.

"Wake me if you need me, but Hayes will take good care of you. And you like my cock too much to let Hayes touch you."

I grin. "True."

I head downstairs and find Hayes flipping something onto a plate. I take a seat at the bar, and Hayes slides the plate in front of me before sitting on the stool next to me.

I pick up the fork and stab at the amazing-looking omelet, but with one whiff of it, I know I'm going to barf again if I eat it. But I don't want to hurt Hayes's feelings or draw any attention to myself.

"What's on your mind?" Hayes asks.

That I'm pregnant with Kit's baby. That I just want to go to the drug store and buy a test and pray that I'm wrong. Stress and a stomach bug caused this, not getting knocked up.

"What are the terms of the deal Lennox made with my father?"

I'm not sure if Hayes knows, but it's the only other thing that will distract me.

Hayes stills.

He knows.

"Tell me," I insist.

"It's not mine to tell."

"But you disagree with him hiding it from me?"

"I do."

"Then tell me. I need to know the truth. I need to know the stakes."

He runs his hand through his long hair and adjusts his glasses. He wants to tell me. He thinks I should know. *What's stopping him?*

"I want to protect him," I say.

Hayes looks at me, trying to see my own secrets.

A beat passes. "Lennox made a deal with your father that in exchange for marrying you and becoming the successor, he had to prove himself worthy of the job."

I nod, but that's not the part I don't know.

"Lennox either has to find and kill your greatest enemy —the man you've been hiding from all this time."

"That's not possible. No one has ever been able to find and stop him."

Hayes nods solemnly.

"And the other?"

"He has to fall in love with you."

I gasp. I never would have expected it from Vincent. I never thought he cared if my husband loved me.

"And if he doesn't?"

"He has one year. An heir would certainly help his cause and might make Vincent reconsider the terms, but other-wise, Lennox will fail."

I frown. "You don't think he could love me?"

Hayes's head dips. "It's not you, but Lennox can't love anyone—not romantically, at least. His past trauma-tized him in a way that prevents him from ever loving again."

"What happened?"

"No, that part of his story I can't tell you. That's for him to decide if he wants to share or not."

"Then, why share any of it if you think there is no hope? So we'll get divorced after the year is up, and I'll have to marry someone else, and Lennox will go back to his old life—"

"No, the terms of the deal don't just mean he'd give up becoming Vincent Corsi's successor. Vincent would have him killed."

I suck in a breath.

We've faced danger and death already. But there is a difference between fighting when attacked and risking your life all to become my husband and Vincent's heir to a group of men who hate you.

Hayes rests his lips together, letting me take it all in. I feel like I'm going to be sick.

I stand up and put my hands over my head, needing more air.

Lennox is going to die.

I'm going to die.

It's just a matter of who outlives whom.

I have accepted my own death—but the thought of Lennox actually dying, of being hunted by my own father...I can't. It just can't happen. Lennox can't die.

Why?

Because I love him.

I love him.

Is that enough to save him?

Will my love be enough to make him love me?

And this baby—will being pregnant ruin any chances at saving our lives?

Then Hayes, as if hearing all my questions, answers them for me. "You can't save him any more than he can save you."

"Why would he agree to those terms?"

"To save Beckett and Ri. To protect all of us. Lennox is a grumpy martyr with the biggest heart. I know you love him, but it won't be enough."

I frown. I have to find a way to make it enough.

CHAPTER 36

Lennox

"YOU LOOK FUCKING INCREDIBLE," I say as I sit across from Rialta at her favorite Italian restaurant.

She smiles in her low-cut black dress that shows off her incredible tits and matches the dark color of her hair. But her smile is what catches my attention the most. She hasn't smiled much this last week.

Probably because I haven't shared anything that's been happening or my deal with Vincent or the truth. I've decided I want to share, but I don't know how.

If we are going to make a real go at a caring relationship, at trying to outlive our short lifespans, then I need to tell her everything. Only then can she decide if she really wants to be with me.

This past week, though, we've been going through the motions, processing everything. I've been trying my best to infiltrate Corsi's ranks, meeting with many of his men. Trying to find spies within the men. Trying to find who I can trust. And most importantly, trying to find dirt on Andrea.

If he is the man responsible for trying to end the Corsi

line, it would make my life a lot easier. But all the dirt I've got on him just leads to him being a young, ambitious, and power-hungry man who thinks he can become the next Corsi leader.

Rialta has spent her days with Hayes and Ri mostly. She went with Beckett to one of Ri's doctor appointments. And Hayes has been continuing to work with her on her self-defense and training.

We've barely spoken during the day this past week, but every evening I've held her close. That is until she woke up and ran to the bathroom, expelled everything in her stomach, and passed out in my arms again.

It worries me—the nightmares.

It's only been a week, but I know the toll that kind of trauma will take on her. And I can't do anything to stop it.

She can try therapy, but that typically doesn't work on people like us. People who have seen the darkest of darks. People who live through death and pain every day.

I worry I pushed her too far.

We haven't had sex since that night. I want her, and I think she wants me, but until we have a conversation, neither of us knows how to initiate it.

But tonight, things will change. I'll tell her everything over dinner—even the parts that Hayes and Gage wouldn't want me to share, and then she can decide what she wants to do.

The waiter pours the wine we ordered and leaves us in peace in the private room I booked.

"To our long and happy future together." I hold up my glass.

She does the same. "To us."

We clink glasses, and I take a long sip.

She doesn't.

I frown. "Are you feeling okay?"

She puts her glass down solemnly. "No, I'm not okay."

My lips tighten into a thin line, and I cock my head. "What's going on?"

In the blink of an eye, deep sobs replace her smile. Tears drip down her face, mascara running along with them. "How could you?"

I frown, my eyebrows pinching together. "How could I do what?"

She chokes on her tears, and I jump up, moving toward her. I kneel in front of her, taking her hands in mine.

"Rialta, talk to me. Tell me what happened. What's wrong?"

I never kneel.

I never beg.

I never let myself care about anyone new—not like I do now.

But whatever answer she gives, I want her to know that I would move mountains and take down every man in the world single-handedly to make whatever pain she's dealing with better.

"Kit," she squeaks out, and my heart stops.

She still loves him.

She still wants him.

And if she does, *she can have him.*

My heart tries to stab me for having that thought, for considering letting her go. *She's mine,* it says.

"Kit," she sobs his name again.

It feels like a stab to my own heart.

Finally, she looks at me with daggers in her eyes. "You killed Kit."

Three simple words and I know I've lost her forever.

Her hands pull from mine as she stands up, pushing her chair back.

I try to stand to talk to her, to tell her the truth, but I can't move.

Why can't I fucking move?

"Well done, Rialta," Andrea says as he enters the spinning room growing foggier by the second.

What the hell?

I force myself to my feet but immediately stumble back.

Andrea says something else, and then he laughs manically, wrapping his arm around Rialta's waist—*my wife's waist!*

She's still sobbing—her eyes are locked on me in disgust as I fall back to the ground. The room becomes darker and darker.

She drugged me—the wine. She put poison in the wine.

My mind races for an answer. *Did she drug me to sedate me or kill me?*

Andrea laughs again and then kisses her cheek.

She doesn't move or deflect him.

Her eyes just darken at me.

I try to hold onto her dark brown eyes. I try to focus on them. To keep them with me. To find some truth that tells me this is a mistake. That she didn't mean to kill me.

But I can't find it.

She's broken—because of me.

My eyes fall shut, unable to stay open any longer.

I force my lips to move, but no sound comes out. I can't speak my truth, but I think it.

I love you, Rialta. And I could have saved us.

———

Thank you for reading Lennox & Rialta's story! I hope you enjoyed it! There story concludes in RIALTA

One-click RIALTA Here

Lennox taught me how strong I really am.
But it backfired on him.
Because now I'm strong enough to take him
and everyone he loves down.
I thought he had a soul—a heart
But he's just the villain.
And I know what to do with villains...

JOIN ELLA'S NEWSLETTER & NEVER MISS A SALE OR NEW RELEASE → ellamiles.com/freebooks

Also by Ella Miles

TRUTH OR LIES:

Taken by Lies #1

Betrayed by Truths #2

Trapped by Lies #3

Stolen by Truths #4

Possessed by Lies #5

Consumed by Truths #6

SINFUL TRUTHS:

Sinful Truth #1

Twisted Vow #2

Reckless Fall #3

Tangled Promise #4

Fallen Love #5

Broken Anchor #6

LIES SERIES:

Lies We Share: A Prologue #0.5

Vicious Lies #1

Desperate Lies #2

Fated Lies #3

Cruel Lies #4

Dangerous Lies #5

Endless Lies #6

RETRIBUTION GAMES SERIES:

Mistaken Hero #1

Forbidden Princess #2

Tempted Hero #3

Fatal Princess #4

Tortured Hero #5

Dangerous Princess #6

RETRIBUTION KINGS SERIES:

Lennox #1

PRETEND SERIES:

Pretend I'm Yours

Pretend We're Over

Pretend: The Complete Series

DIRTY SERIES:

Dirty Obsession

Dirty Addiction

Dirty Revenge

Dirty: The Complete Series

ALIGNED SERIES:

Aligned: Volume 1

Aligned: Volume 2

Aligned: Volume 3

Aligned: Volume 4

Aligned: The Complete Series Boxset

UNFORGIVABLE SERIES:

Heart of a Thief

Heart of a Liar

Heart of a Prick

Unforgivable: The Complete Series Boxset

MAYBE, DEFINITELY SERIES:

Maybe Yes

Maybe Never

Maybe Always

Maybe: The Complete Series

Definitely Yes

Definitely No

Definitely Forever

Definitely: The Complete Series

STANDALONES:

Finding Perfect

Savage Love

Too Much

Not Sorry

Hate Me or Love Me: An Enemies to Lovers Romance Collection

Ella Miles writes steamy romance, including everything from dark suspense romance that will leave you on the edge of your seat to contemporary romance that will leave you laughing out loud or crying. Most importantly, she wants you to feel everything her characters feel as you read.

Ella is currently living her own happily ever after near the Rocky Mountains with her high school sweetheart husband. Her heart is also taken by her goofy five year old black lab who is scared of everything, including her own shadow.

Ella is a USA Today Bestselling Author & Top 50 Bestselling Author.

Stalk Ella at:
www.ellamiles.com
ella@ellamiles.com